Surprised by Grace

Twelve Stories of Lives Changed

TIM ROEHL

PROMISE
PRESS
An Imprint of Barbour Publishing

© 2000 by Tim Roehl

Interior artwork: Mari Goering

ISBN 1-57748-841-5

Published by Promise Press, an imprint of Barbour Publishing, Inc., P.O. Box 719, Uhrichsville, Ohio 44683 www.barbourbooks.com

 Member of the
Evangelical Christian
Publishers Association

Printed in the United States of America.

Dedication

To my Dad—
my first earthly image of a loving Heavenly Father.
Thanks, Dad, for taking us to church
so I could learn about Jesus. . .
for teaching me through your life. . .
and thank you for always encouraging my walk with Him.

Contents

1. *Life-Mender*
   Four friends who bring their paralyzed friend to Jesus find the power of persistent love.

2. *First Called, First Caller*
   The story of two brothers and the One who called them to the greatest adventure life can offer.

3. *Sudden Storm, Stronger Savior*
   A howling storm and a powerful Savior. . .lessons for the storms of our lives.

4. *Showdown in a Graveyard*
   The story of the demoniac among the tombs sets the stage for this drama of spiritual warfare.

5. *Meeting Grace*
   A woman caught in adultery is surprised by grace.

6. *Twelve Unlikely Men*
   A report on Jesus' inner circle of twelve shows how He calls and uses even the most unlikely as His Kingdom-builders.

7. *The Touch of Faith*
   A leper, a desperate father, and a nameless woman find the faith that brings freedom.

8. *Lunch for 20,000*
   Through the eyes of the little boy who gave his lunch, we
   see Jesus' power to provide.

9. *A New Way of Living*
   A woman at a well finds her eyes opened to life beyond
   what she has seen before.

10. *Seeing Lessons from a Blind Man*
    A blind man teaches us how to "see" with faith.

11. *Jesus Comes Late. . .Just in Time*
    The story of Lazarus, Mary, and Martha. . .and the power
    of true faith and resurrection life.

12. *The Short Man's Savior*
    A man trying to measure up meets the One who gives
    him a whole new identity.

Some Words From the Author

You're about to read the stories of real people who lived nearly two millenniums ago. Your first response might be, "So what? That's just ancient history. What would the stories of people who died a long time ago have to do with my life today?"

That's the whole point! History is "His story"—the timeless Story of God at work in people just like you and me no matter what the time, generation, or nation. When God's Story (the story with the big "S") meets the story of someone like you or me (stories with a small "s"), supernatural things can happen! The Jesus who changed the lives of the people we meet in the Bible then is the same Jesus who changes lives now. God still meets us today. . .and lives are forever different.

My hope is that in these stories of people in the Bible you will see your own story. More importantly, you will "see" the main Character of every story and say, "That's the Jesus I want to know." He's changed my life and I know He can change yours.

If you see the real Jesus striding off the pages of Scripture into the heart of your story. . .

If you come to Jesus in simple faith like the people in this book. . .

As you watch His Story intersect with your story. . .

I believe you will find now what they discovered then. . .

Everyone who meets Jesus Christ is changed. . .

Surprised by grace.

Blessings,

Tim

Acknowledgments

So many people made so much difference in making this book a reality. Abundant, grateful thanks to:

- Shirley, my wonderful wife. You've always encouraged my writing dreams. . .you're a great wife, mom, and ministry partner. I love you.
- Aubrey and Elise, our awesome daughters. You've allowed your dad time to write and still made sure we took time to play.
- My mom—an English professor who can review my work with skill and still encourage the way only a mother can.
- My wonderful church families of Grace Chapel in Milwaukee, Wisconsin and ChristLife Evangelical Church in Blaine, Minnesota. You've been a joy to share Christ with. . . your encouragement helped turned these "story sermons" into the stories of this book. Thank you for the privilege of being your pastor.
- The late Rev. Peter Marshall, who first helped me "see" Jesus in print. . .and in my heart.
- Susan Schlabach and the whole team at Barbour Books/ Promise Press. You've made the publishing process a pleasure!
- My editor Ellyn Sanna for your gracious and wise edits. . . you are a delight to work with!
- My secretary Jill Zachor—you're a great ministry help in so many ways.

- Amanda Meckelke, Angie Byrum, and Justin Lefto—for reviewing the unfinished work and giving helpful suggestions.
- The men who graciously reviewed this book—you are my writing heroes!
- My dog Freeway—a scruffy companion who has sat at my side many times as I've written, read, and prayed.

Life-Mender

On his back, he stared up at the ceiling. The first shades of sunrise were filtering into the room through the window, but he had been awake and looking into the darkness for several hours. As the dawn made the four walls and ceiling of his room visible, he faced the pain of another day and the blackness of his own hopelessness.

He knew every crack, every bump in the ceiling by heart—knew them with his eyes closed. For Isaac, every day began in the same position. His paralyzed body wouldn't allow him any other. . .and here on his back he would remain until a friend came to help him wash up, relieve himself, and turn on his side to look at the cracks and bumps of one of the walls. Later, another friend would come to turn him onto his other side to look at another wall, and finally another would prepare him for the night by putting him on his back. His whole life was spent in this small, sparse room. His bed formed the borders of his world.

He had been paralyzed for a long time. Nobody seemed to know why his body had begun to wither and shrivel or why the power to use his arms or to walk had ebbed away from him. Now, although his mind screamed for his limbs to move, they remained twisted and unresponsive. Every passing day pounded the futility and frustration further into his heart. He smiled tightly, remembering that although his name meant "laughter", nothing had brought joy to his life for a long time.

He'd been to doctors. They had checked him thoroughly, suggested treatments, prescribed medicines, and finally shook their heads in defeat at the disease that bound him.

He had tried to see the religious leaders, as well. Perhaps if human means could not help him, divine assistance was possible. But the religious leaders had been unwilling even to see him; sickness, they believed, was always a result of sin. Since he was suffering, he must be merely paying the price for some sin he had committed. "Get rid of your sins," they told him, "and then come to us for help." Yet they had shown him no way to be released from his sins. In the end, they had only reinforced his sense of worthlessness and despair.

He had even tried praying to God, but his prayers seemed to have no more life to them than his paralyzed limbs did. *Maybe God is paralyzed, too,* he thought. Lately, bitterness paralyzed his spirit as much as disease did his body.

Thankfully, he did have friends. His family and the friends he had known since he was a boy stood by him, helped him, and did their best to lift his spirits. Day after day they came, always willing to do the menial and often unpleasant tasks of caring for an invalid. Without them he would have been dead long ago.

The sun was higher now, and he began to feel the warmth of its light. It felt good. He got cold so easily, and the thin cloak that served as his blanket hadn't been enough to keep him warm during the night.

From down the street that ran along the front of his house, he heard the voice of his friend Jacob call out a cheery greeting. *Odd,* he thought. *Jacob doesn't usually come until the evening.* Then he heard the voice of Benjamin. . .and Thomas and James. Several voices were coming toward him, all bubbling with an excitement he had not heard before. Why were all his helpers coming at once?

All four tried to squeeze through the door at the same time, obviously eager to get into the room to see their friend. Their faces glowed with anticipation. "Isaac!" James burst out. "We've got good news for you!"

Isaac couldn't help but be curious, but he'd been let down too many times before to allow his hopes to rise. "What's the news?" he asked wryly. "Have you found a miracle cure for my bedsores?"

"No, my friend," said Thomas, "even better than that! We think we have found a cure for your disease! A Man has come to town who can help you."

"I've seen every doctor there is to see, and I don't want to hear another one tell me there is no hope," responded Isaac, his voice edged with bitterness.

"No, not another doctor," replied Jacob patiently. "This Man is a teacher, a prophet, a good Man. . .and He is a healer. Some are even calling Him the One God promised to send to set us free. Jesus of Nazareth is His name. He has come to our town. . .and we are going to take you to see Him!" The others nodded their heads eagerly.

Isaac had heard about the Carpenter from Nazareth creating such a sensation throughout the region. Many reports told of His powerful teaching and His openness to everyone who came to Him. Isaac had heard that no one who came with a need was turned away. For a moment he considered the words of his friends, but then he moved the few muscles that did work in his body to shake his head slowly. "He won't have time to see me. I'm a nobody. He will have more important people to see."

"No, Isaac. Jesus will see you. We're sure of it." James spoke with quiet resolve.

Thomas knelt down so he could look his friend squarely in the eyes. His own gaze showed dogged determination. "Isaac, you will see Jesus. We will make sure of it. Nothing will stop us!" His look grew more tender. "You've been our friend for years, and you mean too much to us to miss this chance." Then, turning to the others, he said, "Come on, men, let's get going!"

The four men picked up their withered friend by the four corners of the bed that was little more than a flimsy cot. Taking him out the door, they carried him carefully down the street to where Jesus was teaching. The look on Isaac's face showed a mixture of apprehension, fear, pain, and. . .the first glimmer of hope.

When they arrived at the small house where Jesus was

speaking, they saw that people jammed the place full and spilled out into the narrow street halfway down the block. People were straining to hear the words spoken from inside the house even though they couldn't see the Teacher. The words of Jesus, spoken in a strong yet gentle voice, carried to where the four men stood with their burden.

"How are we going to get in there?" whispered James. "There's not enough room for a child much less us. Maybe if we were birds we could fly over their heads and into the room."

For a long moment they stood motionless, silently deciding whether to give up or figure out another way to get to the Teacher. It was one of those life-changing moments when the decision is made either to turn back from a difficult obstacle or to persist; to quit or see it through. Suddenly Thomas looked above the crowd to the roof. A smile broke across his face as he turned to the others. "We may not be birds, brothers, but we can still get over their heads."

Along the side of the house, as with many homes in that area, a stairway led up to the roof. The flat roofs were places to get fresh air and sunshine. The men knew that the beams of the roof would be about three feet apart, covered with brush and then with mud; making a hole in the roof would not be a difficult task. If there was no way through the door, they would make a new door. . .in the form of a skylight.

Slowly, carefully they climbed the steps, straining to keep the bed level. Once on the roof, they paused to listen. Jacob walked over to a spot near one side and said, "Let's dig. . .here." Methodically, in spite of their eager haste, they began to take the roof apart. Their paralyzed friend watched in quiet wonder.

In the crowded room below, a mixture of people listened to

Jesus of Nazareth. Some were common people, nondescript in the crowd, but all felt as if they were noticed and valued by the Teacher. Here and there a man stood with his hands on the shoulders of a child standing in front of him. Near the front, in the seats of greatest prominence, sat a row of robed religious leaders. From their expressions, they were obviously not there to listen to Jesus. Instead, they were there to critique . . .and to criticize. . .and hopefully to condemn the Man in front of them. They couldn't explain the miracles taking place wherever Jesus went, but they didn't like them.

Suddenly, dust and small chunks of dirt began to fall from the ceiling. All eyes turned upward at this unexpected source of distraction, and some people brushed the dust from their hair. Jesus stopped speaking and looked up with quizzical amusement. All attention now focused on the growing hole in the ceiling. For a few moments there was no sound but that of the roof being dismantled.

Now the hole in the ceiling between the two beams was about six feet long, and sunlight fell in a bright rectangle on the floor below, directly in front of Jesus. Four heads appeared against the sky above,

Many parts of Israel were rocky, with not many trees. Wood was scarce, so most homes were small, built with stones and clay. Rainfall was also sparse, so a flat roof was often used. In a small house with little extra space, the roof was used as a place for rest and relaxation; most houses had outside steps or a ladder to reach the rooftop.

The easiest way to put a hole through a roof like this would have been to dig out the roofing between the beams. It would not damage the house much, and it would be easy to repair.

looking down into the room. Their eyes were bright, expectant, as they searched for one particular person.

"Jesus of Nazareth?"

The strong, tanned face of the Carpenter smiled up at them. "Yes. I'm here."

Four pairs of eyes lit up with joy! "We have someone we want you to meet," one of the men said gruffly. "He is our friend. . .and he needs Your help. Wait. . . ." The man's head withdrew. "We'll lower him to You. His name is Isaac."

A bed came slowly down through the hole in the roof until it rested gently on the floor. Isaac looked up at the crowd. Tension filled the room. All eyes were now on the paralyzed man and the Carpenter.

Isaac lay on his side in front of Jesus. For a moment he could not bring himself to look up into His face. Whether fear or guilt held him back Isaac couldn't tell, but he knew he was in the presence of Someone different than he had ever met before. He couldn't meet Jesus' eyes.

But then Jesus leaned forward. "Isaac," He said softly, gently. "Isaac, look at Me."

Slowly, Isaac raised his eyes. The face above him came as a surprise; Jesus looked ordinary enough, like any other Jewish man. And yet something about the look in His eyes lit a spark of hope deep within Isaac's heart. Tenderness, openness, acceptance, all shone in those eyes. Neither man spoke for a moment. . .but their two hearts communicated. One told of years of unspoken fears and dreams, pain and need; and the other answered with understanding and kindness, invitation and grace. Jesus looked past the shriveled limbs of Isaac's body and saw the aching need of his heart.

Jesus looked up again at the four faces still above Him, all pleading silently for Him to help their friend. Then, slowly and confidently, Jesus looked at Isaac and said, "Son, your sins are forgiven."

An audible gasp whispered through the room. The words were so unexpected that people were not sure they had heard correctly. They struggled to make sense of what the Carpenter had just said to Isaac. In the silent room, their thoughts were almost audible: *Forgive sin? Unheard of! No ordinary man has the authority to forgive sin. . .that belongs to God alone. This is strange. . .*

illegal. . .

unless. . .

unless the Man who spoke the words is more than just a man. He would have to be the Messiah to say something like that.

He would have to be God.

The crowd's conclusion was not lost on the robed religious leaders, and their eyes glowed with anger. They began to mutter and look at each other with expressions of wounded religious pride and righteous indignation. This was blasphemy! It was a crime punishable by death. How dare this plain Carpenter and pretend prophet elevate Himself to the level of Almighty God!

Isaac neither heard nor sensed any of this. His eyes had grown wide at the gift of forgiveness Jesus had just handed to him. Somehow. . .somehow this Carpenter knew his real need. He knew about the bitterness, the anger, the self-pity, the whole sordid mess that had warped Isaac's soul and paralyzed his heart. Jesus had spoken to Isaac's real need, and now, for the first time, Isaac knew freedom. He felt washed clean, released from the disease of sin that had held him captive so long. His body had not changed outwardly, but his heart was dancing with joy. Tears ran down his cheeks and onto his beard, then dropped in smudges on the dirty mattress, while thankfulness shone from his face.

Jesus smiled at his new friend, quiet joy on His face at the response He saw in Isaac's heart.

He looked up at the row of religious leaders, and His expression changed. He knew what they were thinking; He knew the narrowness and pettiness of their hearts, and for a moment, anger flashed in His eyes. They would rather keep their precious religious traditions than help this needy man. Their coldness pained and angered Him, and they looked away under his unwavering gaze.

After a moment, however, His face softened a bit, and a hint of amusement played at the corners of His mouth. Speaking loud enough so all could hear, He said to the row of leaders, "I know what you're thinking. You're thinking only God can forgive sins. But what's more important? To forgive and set a man free from his sins—or to heal his body? You believe a man is sick because he sinned. Well, if we're going to heal the sickness, we'll have to forgive the sin first, won't we?" His eyes twinkled. The rest of the people in the room grasped His simple logic, and heads nodded as people nudged each other.

Jesus continued. "You may say that it is easy to speak of forgiveness—but impossible to tell if the work has really been done. So all right, men, to show you that the Son of Man has power to forgive sins, I'll show you the evidence."

His eyes still twinkling, Jesus turned back to Isaac. Then He smiled and said in a strong, glad voice, "Isaac, pick up your bed and go home."

Isaac's eyes grew even wider. No one had ever said such a thing to him! His heart was now free, but could his body ever work again? Quickly, he came to a decision: He would try to do what Jesus asked, no matter what.

As soon as the choice was made in his heart, he felt life and strength surging through his withered limbs. His arms straightened out; his fingers untwisted and began to flex. His legs, curled up to his chest, stretched out to their full length. New muscle appeared instantly. Shoulders straightened; toes wiggled. He could move! He could move!

Rolling over onto all fours, he put his feet under him and sprang up. He could stand!

He took a step. . .

then another. . .

then a hop. . .

and suddenly Isaac danced in the light that shone through the hole above, clapping his hands, tears of joy streaming down his face, as he shouted with glee. He grinned up at the faces of his friends.

Jesus stood, His eyes glistening with tears as He watched the man in front of Him. He looked up at the faces of Isaac's four friends, and they stared back at Him, speechless, their faces wet with tears of joy and gratitude.

The crowd exploded! A cheer rang though the room. A miracle. A miracle had been performed in front of their eyes. This Man, this Carpenter, this Teacher, this Healer, this Forgiver, was more than just a man. He was a Life-Mender!

Isaac stopped dancing long enough to look again at his new Master and Friend. Spontaneously, he and Jesus gave each other a hug, Isaac's head resting on Jesus' strong shoulder as a child would rest his head on his parent's. Then Jesus put His hands on Isaac's shoulders and looked into his eyes. "Isaac, pick up your bed and go home with your friends."

Tears still running down his cheeks, Isaac picked up his bed and danced out of the house and down the street, through a corridor of amazed people.

He laughed with his friends all the way home.

Surprised by grace, everything Isaac thought he knew about God was forever changed when he met Jesus for himself. Our misconceptions are changed when we meet the real Jesus for ourselves, too. For example, our Lord has a sense of humor! Where did we get the concept of the dark, brooding, stoic Jesus? Or where did we develop the misconception of a weak, mild, and spineless Christ? The real Jesus, though He was "a man of sorrows and familiar with suffering," brought joy wherever He went. The Jesus we see walking through the pages of the New Testament was a Man who was also familiar with laughter. He's fun to be around. In fact, Jesus permeates life with joy.

Thank God for the "Hole in the Roof Gang"—those four wonderful friends. Be grateful for those who have loved you enough to bring you to Jesus, who cared so much that they wouldn't leave you in your present situation. But also remember that when they "lay you at the feet of Jesus," they can do no more for you; from there it's up to you to either stay on your bed of weakness and unwillingness—or respond to Christ.

So often we look only on the outside appearance of things — when all the while Jesus is wanting to make us whole not only on the outside, but on the inside, too. Jesus knows the real needs of our life; He always starts with the heart, because our heart is where all the other issues of life find their origin. So often we try to put a Flintstone Band-Aid on our broken hearts, hoping our deep wounds will be covered with superficial human effort.

Jesus has the power to bring healing to every area of our lives: emotional, mental, physical, spiritual, relational. His life-mending grace makes everything whole again. He made our original design, and even when we are wounded by our own sin or the effects of its curse, Jesus knows how to put us back together again.

Jesus knows your situation. He knows all the times you tried and saw no visible results. He knows your frustration. But the Life-Mender is not deterred. When you reach out to Him in simple, even faltering faith, Jesus will make you whole. You'll find what Isaac did so long ago. . .

and what people just like us still find today. . .

the Life-Mender does all things well.

BEYOND THE STORY
Questions to Nudge Your Thinking
and Nourish Your Heart

1. Why do you think our world has often pictured Jesus as either dark and brooding—or weak and wimpy? Why might we be uncomfortable with a strong and joyful Jesus?

2. What part of your life feels broken lately? Have you offered it up to Jesus for His healing?

3. When we want to be whole and yet we seem to stay broken, year after year, what should we do?

4. Do you have any friends like Isaac's? Have you asked them to help you come to Jesus for healing?

5. Jesus is looking for more members of His "Hole in the Roof Gang." He loves people with faith that laughs at barriers. Who can you help bring to Jesus?

First Called, First Caller

*A*ndrew squinted as he looked out across the waters of the Sea of Galilee. The sun made brilliant diamonds across the lake's blue surface, and beneath the sparkling waves swam their livelihood. *Now,* he thought, *if we can just find them, net them, and haul them into our boat, those fish will pay for more than just our daily bread.*

However, being a fisherman on this unpredictable harp-shaped bowl of water wasn't easy work, and their scaly prey was not cooperating today. Andrew looked over at his big brother

Simon pulling in yet another empty net and smiled. Simon. . . impulsive, brash, loud. Sometimes he got them into trouble with his big mouth, but one thing Simon didn't do was give up easily. He had been pulling in empty nets all day, yet he was still trying. The sea breeze gently blew Simon's bushy beard and wispy hair as he glanced up at his brother.

"What are you looking at, grinning at me like that?" Simon gave him a wry look. "You've been even quieter than usual, Andrew. What are you thinking about now?"

"Ever feel like your life is as empty as that net, my brother?" Andrew's voice was quiet and thoughtful. Simon's only answer was a roll of his eyes as he continued pulling in the net.

"No, seriously, Simon. We've been in this fishing business with James and John for years now, and our fathers were in this business before that. I like being a fisherman, but lately it just seems, well. . .it just seems like there's got to be more to life than this."

> In the time of Jesus, the Sea of Galilee was thick with fishing boats. There were three methods of fishing: First was line fishing. Second was fishing with the casting net, a circular net that might be as much as nine feet across. It was cast into the water from the land or from the shallow water at the edge of the lake, weighted with pellets of lead round the circumference. It sank into the sea and surrounded the fish, and it was then drawn through the water as if the top of a bell tent were being drawn to land, the fish caught inside. The third method, the drag net, was used from a boat, or better from two boats. It was cast into the water with ropes at each of the four corners, weighted at the foot so that it would stand upright in the water. When the boats were rowed along with the net behind them, the net became a great cone to catch the fish.
>
> ∾

Simon waved a big calloused hand at Andrew. "I know what's gotten into you. . .you've been hearing about that prophet down south of here. Look, little brother, preachers come and preachers go, so what's special about this John they call the Baptizer? You make a decent living here, there's food on our tables, our families are in good health. What more do you want?"

Andrew hesitated before he answered. He had grown up in the shadow of his older brother, who usually spoke first and thought later. Andrew, who had gotten used to being inconspicuous, was the one who tended to wait until he had something to say before he said anything. With his boisterous personality, Simon got the most attention when they were in the crowd, but Andrew had learned the art of making others feel comfortable by listening well and speaking wisely.

He watched his brother expertly toss the circular net out across the water and wait until it began to settle beneath the waves. Then he said, "I'm not sure if I can explain it, Simon, but it's like I've got this empty place in my heart that seems to be getting bigger and emptier the older I get. I know our parents raised us to be religious. . .somehow I feel that only God can fill this emptiness—and I haven't found Him yet. If. . .if this John the Baptizer really is a prophet who comes from God, or if he's actually the Messiah our people have been waiting for, then maybe he can show me how to find what I'm searching for. Does that make sense?"

Simon, for once, looked at his brother thoughtfully for a long moment before he spoke. "I think I can understand what you are saying, Andrew," he said at last. "One thing I do know for sure is that you haven't been much help around here lately.

The fish haven't been cooperating much either, so I'll tell you what. Why don't you take a trip to hear this John the Prophet or Baptizer or Messiah or whatever he is and get this out of your system." With a twinkle in his eye, he added, "Besides, who knows? You may be onto something after all. As for me. . .well, I'll stick to catching fish until something better comes along."

Soon Andrew was on the road headed south to the barren land near the Jordan River. John the Baptizer, as he had become known, was drawing people here from all over the country to hear his passionate call to repent and receive God's forgiveness. The crowds were impressed with John's utter disregard for social, political, religious, or military position as he dealt specifically and directly with people from all those walks of life.

John's call to be baptized bypassed racial or religious backgrounds; it was a call to the heart. Every man or woman, preached John, was equally invited to repent and receive God's forgiveness in simple faith. When Andrew joined the crowds around John, he soon realized that John's message came directly from God. Andrew was spellbound as he listened. This man not only knew *about* God; he *knew* God!

John's invitation to be baptized as an outward sign of an inward work of God was an unusual idea for any Jew. Israelites were never baptized; as God's chosen people, they felt they already belonged to God and no further spiritual cleansing was needed. Only foreigners from other religions who were converting to Judaism were baptized. . .until John. John's ministry was different in many ways from the normal message and method of a priest, even though John was the son of a priest. His was a ministry uniquely given by God.

Andrew wished he could talk personally with John. Maybe—just maybe—John had the answers to the questions swirling in Andrew's heart. Andrew wanted to know God the way John knew Him. He decided he would wait until the crowd left and see if John would take time to talk with him.

That night when at last the crowds headed home, Andrew shyly came alongside John as the prophet began his solitary journey deeper into the wilderness. "May I walk with you. . . and perhaps ask you some questions?" Andrew's query was soft but earnest.

John looked over at him as they continued walking. Earlier in the day his eyes had glowed with intensity as he preached, but now his gaze was surprisingly gentle. "I see in you a seeking heart, my friend. If you don't mind locusts and honey for your meal, I'd be happy to have your company."

Thus began the friendship of the two men. Before long Andrew stood with John in the cool waters of the Jordan River. Confessing his desire to follow God, he knelt as John placed his hand on Andrew's head; Andrew bowed his heart and body until he was fully covered by the water. Andrew knew something was different inside him, and his yearning to know God increased.

He became John's follower and helper, greeting and guiding the people as they came to hear the Baptizer. John's popularity grew daily. The crowds continued to swell as seekers as well as skeptics journeyed to the banks of the Jordan River to hear John preach his message of repentance.

Andrew noticed, however, that John always drew attention away from himself, as if he were preparing the way for someone else. Finally, a few weeks after Andrew began following John, he worked up the courage to ask what was for him the all-important question. "Are. . .are you the Messiah? Are you the Promised One God has sent to redeem His people?"

John looked at him with his clear, piercing eyes. "No, I am not. I'm just preparing the way for the One who is far greater than I am. I am not even fit to untie the laces on His sandals. When He comes, He will baptize, not with water, but with the Holy Spirit and with fire!" Then, looking down the road, John's eyes suddenly lit up, his excitement plain on his face. Pointing to a Man coming toward them, he exclaimed, "Andrew. . .there is the One I've been talking about. Behold. . .the Lamb of God who takes away the sins of the world."

For a moment John's words hung in the air, catching Andrew by surprise. *The Lamb of God. . .*For any Jew, the words

The Passover Lamb was a vital part of the Israelites' deliverance when they were slaves in Egypt. On one incredible night, spotless lambs were sacrificed in Jewish homes all over the land. Blood from the lambs was smeared over the doorposts as an act of protective faith. That night God's angel of death moved across the land in judgment, taking the life of every first born, human and animal alike, from every dwelling place. . .except for those homes covered by the blood. The lifeblood of the lamb became the Jews' lifesaver.

In Andrew's day, at the Temple in Jerusalem, lambs were sacrificed morning and evening for the sins of the people. Blood flowed over the altar, a reminder of the consequences of sin, reassuring humble hearts of God's holy standards and yet His willingness to forgive.

During the days when the Jews' struggle against Roman rule was led by Judas Maccabees, a horned lamb was the symbol of a great conqueror, a champion of God who would bring victory to His people. Some believed that the Lamb of God would fight God's enemies and overcome them in a single conquest. Every faithful Israelite knew the "Lamb of God" was a description of God's Messiah. . .the answer to every yearning heart hungry to truly know God.

had tremendous spiritual implications. Andrew thought of the Passover Lamb that was such a vital part of bringing them freedom when they were slaves in Egypt. Passages from the Scriptures came to Andrew's thoughts: the prophet Jeremiah writing, "But I was like a gentle lamb led to the slaughter;" Isaiah speaking of One who was like a lamb to the slaughter. Both men wrote as if seeing ahead down the corridors of time to the one Person who would become a spotless, sinless sacrifice—the Messiah.

John had called this Man the Lamb of God.

Dressed in the simple garb of a tradesman, the Man did not appear to be anyone extraordinary. As He drew closer, Andrew could see the strength in His arms and the calluses on His hands. *Odd,* he thought, *for the Messiah to look so. . .ordinary.*

It was then Andrew saw the Man's face. His features were ordinary enough, but when Andrew's eyes met His, he was startled by the knowing gaze that silently indicated He had been expecting Andrew. The acceptance in those eyes encouraged Andrew to approach Him.

The Man grabbed John in a big hug. Then, turning to Andrew, John said, "Andrew, I want you to meet Jesus of Nazareth."

Jesus reached out His hand and greeted Andrew with a firm handclasp and a welcoming smile.

"Rabbi, where are you staying?" As he blurted the question, Andrew realized he was acting more like Simon, for the question came out of Andrew's mouth before he thought. His few words held meaning. "Rabbi" meant "my great one" and "teacher." "Where are you staying?" was an accepted way to say to someone "I want to get to know you better." Andrew's words were polite, but the message behind his words spoke of a heart that ached with longing. Jesus' reply was simple.

"Come," He said, "and you will see."

Andrew went with Jesus to the place where He was staying and spent the day with Him. All the questions that had been stored up in Andrew's heart poured out, one after the other. Jesus listened closely and answered patiently every inquiry. The more Jesus spoke, the more Andrew could feel the empty places in his soul being filled with something he could not describe; he just knew that Jesus had that for which his heart hungered. He felt as though his parched spirit was taking a long refreshing drink. The two talked late into the evening, and when he finally laid his head on his pillow, Andrew was so excited and overwhelmed that sleep was a long time coming. *At long last,* he thought, *I've found the One I've been looking for. I've got to tell Simon!*

When morning came, Andrew asked Jesus if He would come visit his village and meet his family and friends. Graciously, Jesus consented. Giving Jesus directions, Andrew hurried ahead to prepare for his honored Guest.

The first thing Andrew did when he arrived back at his village was to run to the shoreline, scanning the water for their boat. Spotting the distinctive colors of their sail, Andrew waved and called until he caught his brother's attention. As he helped Simon pull their boat up on the stones of the shore, Andrew could barely contain his excitement. "Simon!" Andrew blurted. "I've found Him. I've found the One we've been looking for. . . and He's coming to visit us!"

Simon grinned at his brother, cocking his head to one side quizzically. Putting up his hands, he smiled and said, "Whoa, slow down, my brother! Why all this excitement? Who have you found that has made such an impression on you?"

Andrew restrained himself with effort and took a deep breath before he replied. "Simon, I believe I've found the One who can help us find God. I've found the Messiah. His name is Jesus. I knew you would need to meet Him, so I've invited Him to come and visit us. When you hear Him and get to know Him, you'll feel the same way I do!"

Seeing the sincerity in his brother's eyes, Simon nodded slowly. "Yes, Andrew, I believe I'd like to meet this Jesus, too."

Several days later when Jesus came walking down the beach, He invited them to become "fishers of men"—and neither of the brothers hesitated. They got up from their nets and followed Jesus, ready to enter the adventure of their lives. From then on, netting fish from the Sea of Galilee would never compare to the exhilaration of leading men and women to meet Jesus the Christ.

When he came home to tell Simon about Jesus, that was the first time Andrew invited someone to meet Christ—but it would not be the last. While Simon (whom Jesus nicknamed Peter) became better known and had a more visible public ministry, Andrew was the one always finding people and personally introducing them to his Savior. His life is a powerful reminder that God is not looking for outstanding ability or charismatic personality; Andrew was the first one Jesus called to follow Him, and he became the one who would be the first to call others to follow Christ, too. If not for the personal, unpretentious ministry of Andrew, Peter's prominent public ministry might never have existed. When Andrew found Jesus had filled the empty net of his heart, he made sure that when it came to fishing for souls, his net would never be empty again.

Jesus is still looking for men and women willing to throw out nets of love to bring hurting hearts to Him. It's a lifetime job with benefits that are out of this world.

Interested?

BEYOND THE STORY
Questions to Nudge Your Thinking
and Nourish Your Heart

1. Research indicates that about 95% of all Christians don't actively share their faith. Most feel they don't "have the right personality." What are some other reasons that hinder Christians from sharing their faith?

2. What can we learn from Andrew when it comes to our own spiritual seeking? What was he willing to do that made his search successful?

3. Andrew first reached out to those he knew best—his friends and family. What natural relational bridges can you use to reach out in love?

4. Others may get more publicity and be more widely applauded, but an "Andrew" knows that all of heaven rejoices when one person comes to Christ. That's the kind of applause an "Andrew" listens for. Who can you introduce to Jesus?

Sudden Storm, Stronger Savior

A day filled with heavenly deeds had suddenly turned into a night of hellish disaster.

It had started out as an ordinary morning. Jesus and His disciples had set out to Peter and Andrew's hometown for a visit. Peter was expecting nothing more than a chance to catch up with his wife and family, who he hadn't seen for a while, not since he had been on the road with Jesus. He knew, of course, that any day with Jesus could hold unexpected adventure. That was one of the things that made being His follower so exciting;

He could take an ordinary day and suddenly make it supernaturally extraordinary.

This day was no exception. When they arrived at Peter's home, they found Peter's mother-in-law flushed with a high fever, unable to get out of bed. Peter's wife clung to him with large frightened eyes. They both knew that high fevers in their land were often fatal. Her mother was in great danger.

Instinctively, Peter's eyes turned toward Jesus. He had traveled with Him only a few months, but he had seen Him in many situations; he had never seen Him appear surprised or overwhelmed by anything. Jesus was always in control of any circumstance they encountered, and His calm but concerned face reassured Peter now.

Jesus gave the shoulder of Peter's wife a gentle squeeze of comfort, and then He walked over to the bed where the sick woman moved restlessly. For a moment, He looked intently into the sick woman's eyes, as if He were looking past the physical fever. The room was electric with suspense, every eye riveted on the pair. Then, taking her hand, Jesus spoke firmly, not to the woman, but to the fever: "Leave this woman's body!"

The old woman's dull, fevered eyes grew large with wonder. Suddenly the sparkle of health shone from them, taking years off her appearance. Her entire body relaxed, and her labored breathing slowed. She breathed deeply and freely again. Her skin now radiated health.

With His hand still holding hers, Jesus smiled and beckoned the woman to stand with Him. As she did, everyone in the house gasped in wonder. Her face broke into a huge smile. "I haven't felt so good in years!"

Peter's wife ran to her mother and they clung to each other, sobbing tears of relief and joy. The household, which had been tense and quiet a moment before, suddenly erupted into noisy celebration. Everyone talked at once, trying to comprehend the miracle they had just witnessed. Someone ran out the door to the neighbor's house, and soon the news of the miracle was on the lips of everyone in town. Before long, the entire town seemed to be at Peter's doorstep. After all, when miracles are available, everyone wants to join the party, and the party was at Peter's. His mother-in-law, now the center of delighted attention, began to serve Jesus and His disciples, as well as the uninvited but welcome guests.

Obviously their day of quiet family visiting was gone, replaced by a house full of needy hearts, an exciting opportunity for ministry. A line of people formed to where Jesus sat, and He greeted each person as if he or she were the only person He was going to talk to all day. With a word or a touch He healed sick people and rebuked evil spirits. As Peter watched in wonder, the words of the ancient prophet Isaiah came to his mind: *"He took up our infirmities and carried our diseases."* The prophecy regarding the Messiah was coming to life before Peter's eyes.

Hours passed. The line of people kept Jesus so busy He didn't even have time to eat, but everyone Jesus touched went home with hearts fully satisfied. People formerly bound by disease or darkness joyfully described their newfound freedom to everyone who would listen.

The crowd inside and outside Peter's house continued to grow. Some came to watch skeptically. Others came eager to tell Jesus their problems and find help. Some came with questions.

As Peter watched Jesus, he saw His Master and Friend grow tired from the constant press of the people. Catching Peter's eye, Jesus motioned for him to come near. "Can you get your boat ready to sail?" He whispered in Peter's ear. Nodding, Peter grabbed Andrew and they got their small fishing vessel ready. If they left the village and crossed the lake, they could have a time of quiet.

Minutes later, Jesus came walking down to the water's edge with the rest of the disciples, people still crowding around Him. Bidding the crowd good-bye with a promise to return soon, Jesus got in the boat, and Peter cast off. He and the other men rowed into the setting sun on water as smooth as glass.

The water glowed orange and red as the day's last light reflected off the surface. The thirteen men were silent, the only noise the splash of their oars. After a moment, Jesus, weary from a heavy day of ministry, put his head down on a cushion that Peter knew smelled of fish and promptly went to sleep.

Peter smiled. On land, Jesus was clearly in charge, but here on the water, they were in Peter's domain. Like five of the other twelve disciples, he was an experienced fisherman who had sailed the lake nearly all his life. The boat was in good hands; they were only a short trip from rest on the other side of the lake.

The Sea of Galilee is one of the most picturesque bodies of water in the world. Over twelve miles long and ranging from four to over seven miles wide, it is an oblong harp-shaped bowl of water fed by the rapidly descending Jordan River. Over seven hundred feet below the level of the Mediterranean Sea just twenty-seven miles to the west, the lake is surrounded by hills and cliffs, making its long and narrow shape a funnel for both water. . .and wind.

The Sea of Galilee had a reputation for two things: abundant fish populations and deadly storms that could spring up out of nowhere. The hills around the sea formed a wind tunnel, and the surface could turn from smooth swells to savage thirty-foot waves in a matter of minutes.

It was, Peter thought, a beautiful end to an incredible day.

About halfway across the lake, suddenly eerie dark clouds loomed overhead. James and John noticed them first, and then the other sailors in the boat. The disciples were familiar with dark clouds, of course, but these were unlike any they had ever seen. With unearthly inky blackness, they boiled angrily from within, making them seem alive. This was no ordinary storm. Something else was going on here. They looked at each other with growing uneasiness and rowed harder.

When the wind came seconds later, it struck with such savage fury that the first blast nearly capsized the boat. The water turned as black as the sky above, and huge waves slammed the side of the boat punishing it relentlessly. Lightning exploded from the clouds, thunder boomed instantaneously on its heels, and a sudden icy downpour drenched them. In the space of but a minute, their situation had turned from delightful to deadly.

As the boat pitched and rolled, the disciples who weren't used to sailing turned green. Those who were accustomed to the water turned white; they knew they were still miles from shore.

The wind's howl rose to a shriek, as though hell itself had broken loose on them. The men shouted at each other, but the wind whipped the words from their mouths and carried them away. They couldn't hear each other, but in the lightning flashes, they read the horror on each other's faces. When the waves began to pour in over the sides of the boat, they knew all was lost.

At this terrifying moment, Peter glanced to the back of the boat: Jesus was still asleep! *How in the world can He be asleep at a time like this?* Peter wondered. The other disciples followed his gaze, and for a moment they all paused their frantic activity, watching their Leader, drenched by the storm but peacefully sleeping. The look on His face was the exact opposite of theirs. He was clearly oblivious to their jeopardy.

Crawling over two other men, Peter fought the violent rolling of the boat to get to Jesus. Falling on his knees, he grabbed Jesus by the shoulders and shook Him. "Master, don't You care about us?" he screamed. "We are all going to die! Help us. . .save us!"

If ever Peter would have expected to see Jesus overwhelmed, now was the moment. But Jesus' face never changed when He opened His eyes and saw the panic on Peter's face. He didn't look afraid at all. Instead, as He glanced from the sky to the sea, He looked angry. . .not at them, Peter realized, but at the storm!

Standing up in the boat, the worst thing a person could do in the middle of a storm, Jesus pointed His finger into the storm's howling fury, and shouted, "Calm down! Be quiet!"

The effect was like someone turning off a switch. The wind, howling at gale force, suddenly stopped without a hint of a breeze. The clouds, which had absorbed every bit of light, split apart and disappeared, revealing the sun again. The waves, thirty-foot walls of water, calmed down as they were commanded. The surface of the water became completely still and flat. The only sound now was the water dripping off their hair and clothes onto the boat's deck. Peace ruled.

Their minds needed a moment to catch up. They were still in shock, overwhelmed by the abrupt transition from imminent death to immediate rescue. A couple of them shook their heads, trying to shake away the confusion, spraying drops of water in all directions. All of them looked at Jesus, their mouths hanging open in amazement. They were all thinking the same thing, though no one could bring himself to say it out loud: *Who is this Man? Even the wind and the waves obey Him. Just when we thought we understood Him, He goes and does something like this! Who is He?*

The face of Jesus, hardened like a warrior's in battle a moment before, relaxed. Looking down at His men, He couldn't suppress a grin. What a comical, confused, completely drenched bunch!

For a long minute they stood looking at each other, the disciples staring openmouthed at Jesus and Jesus looking back at them in amusement. Then His smile faded, and He shook His head sadly. After a day of constant miracles in the physical and spiritual realms, some wind and waves were enough to make them act as if God didn't exist at all. The sudden storm had uncovered the smallness of their faith. When a miracle happened in front of them, their faith was in what they could see, not in the One who had created the miracle. Fear had easily overcome their ability to trust Jesus. They were a long way from being ready to do His work.

Jesus' words showed both His disappointment and His love. "Men. . .where is your faith? Don't you trust Me? Why are you so afraid?"

His question stayed with them long after they had reached shore on the other side of the lake and gone to sleep that night.

Many centuries have come and gone since that faith-building trip on the Sea of Galilee, but the same principles apply to us as we encounter the storms of our lives. The storms are like monsters that threaten to overwhelm and consume us—and sudden disaster is a monster most all of us face at one time in our lives, sometimes more than once.

What do we do when the monsters attack us? We can drown in fear—or come out with a stronger faith. The difference depends on where we place our trust.

Jesus asks us the same question He asked His disciples that day on the Sea of Galilee: "Where is your faith?" When we trust Jesus, no storm can overcome us. When He is in charge of our life, our ship will not sink. The storm will not last.

Sudden storms will come, but the next time you are caught in one, stand tall and speak into your situation with faith.

Watch fear retreat.

Watch His peace rule.

BEYOND THE STORY
*Questions to Nudge Your Thinking
and Nourish Your Heart*

1. Satan will attempt to overwhelm us with subtle allurement or sudden attacks. What situations have you faced that seemed designed to capsize your faith?

2. *"On land, Jesus was clearly in charge, but here on the water, they were in Peter's domain."* Do you have areas of your life where you feel so competent and "in control" that you don't need God's help? What lessons can you learn from this story?

3. What can happen to our faith if we focus on God's miracles (what He does) instead of God the Miracle-maker (Who He is)? What are some ways you can stay focused on who Christ is instead of what He can do?

4. Jesus took authority over the storm with His power. He has given us the authority to use His power in simple faith. What "storm" do you need to speak to in your life right now?

Showdown in a Graveyard

haz knew He was coming before he ever saw Him.

The voices inside him all started talking at once, and they were terrified. They had been angry, confused, demanding, leering, taunting at times, but never terrified like this. Somehow Ahaz knew that Someone stronger than the forces that possessed him was coming. . .and now he was either going to die or he was going to be completely free. He knew there would be no middle ground or compromise.

As the sudden storm on the Sea of Galilee grew fiendishly

fierce, the storm inside of him intensified at the same time. When the storm outside supernaturally stopped, there was a sudden shift inside his own spirit. He had been living in the graveyard for many months, but he had lost track of time long ago. His whole life had been lost in darkness—but when light broke through the clouds after that storm, the first glimmer of hope in years broke through his consciousness. A spark of curiosity, a remnant of his own personality, drove him out of his filthy place among the tombs to the shore to see what was going on.

Long ago, the last thing Ahaz would have expected was to find himself in the demonic darkness where he now lived. He had been an average man with a family, living in a small town just off the shore of the Sea of Galilee, no different from other men in his town. He worshipped his work, worked at his play, and played at his worship. He had felt completely in control of his own life—but he was actually a captive to his greed and pride. Yes, unfortunately, Ahaz had

Because Israel was so rocky, burial normally took place in two ways: Burial vaults were carved out of the soft limestone of the region with niches inside the door for separate bodies. Whole families would be laid to rest in the caves over the course of time. The other method was to bury people in a stone coffin above ground. As people visited the graves to remember the dead or pray, they would leave stones on top of the coffins as a sign of their visit. Ahaz probably made his home in a cave among corpses and cut himself with the prayer stones left on coffins by others. For the Jews of the day, anyone who lived in proximity to dead bodies would be "unclean," unable to live among others until he could prove he had been cleansed and restored to physical and spiritual health.

been like many men in his town. At least in the beginning.

His downward slide began with complacency. Although he had grown up with religious values, he had drifted away from placing any real importance on the things of God. His attendance at worship happened whenever it was convenient—or his wife nagged him into going. He never seemed to have time to study God's Word, and prayer was an occasional request for help when he was in trouble. As his spiritual complacency grew, so did the spiritual emptiness in his life.

One day a friend told him about a woman who claimed to be able to tell the future. "It is amazing," his friend said, "what she knows about me that nobody else knows."

Ahaz's complacency turned into curiosity. He went to see the woman.

His friend was right. The woman was amazing in an eerie way. When she looked at Ahaz through the haze of incense, her power was inviting and seductive. Her eyes were dark. . .and empty. Yet Ahaz felt strangely attracted to her words.

After a few more visits, he found himself even more attracted to her spiritual and physical wiles. He did things, things he thought he could control. They seemed exciting. . . so alluring, so satisfying. Ahaz felt like he possessed power now he had only dreamed of before.

But before he realized, his curiosity had made him a captive to dark forces beyond his control. They drew him deeper and deeper down a spiral of perversion and spiritual chaos. What had at first satisfied him now strangled him. Ahaz, whose name means "one who possesses," found himself possessed. His life began to unravel around him. He lost his job. . .his home. . .his family. . .and finally his sanity. More and more, the dark forces took over his mind and body, as though the doorway he had opened to the darkness was thrown open to dozens, hundreds, and finally thousands of demons.

They drove him out of town to the putrid region of the tombs. He was drawn to death, and his eyes now carried the same darkness he had seen in the woman psychic. His body was a naked mass of wounds and infection, and his mind alternated between rage, terror, and utter chaos. The voices. . .he could not stop the voices!

His friends tried to help him. After he began terrorizing other people and slashing himself with sharp objects, they bound him, but with superhuman fury he ripped away the cords and disappeared into the darkness again. Day and night his screams echoed across the hills, shrieks of torment and utter hopelessness.

Then came the day of the storm. . .and the arrival of the Son of God. Through bloodshot, crazed eyes Ahaz saw the fishing boat arrive on the beach. He saw the men get out. . .and one Man suddenly came sharply into focus. Behind the mass of spirits, the person of Ahaz still lived in his body, but he was like a man trapped beneath ice who struggles to find a hole to get his head above water. Somehow, though, Ahaz knew this Man could help him.

The demons in him erupted in terror as Ahaz stumbled toward the Man. *NO! NO! Stay away from this Man! This is no ordinary Man. . .this is the Son of the Most High God!* But all the while the demons shrieked, Ahaz's own voice was crying out: *Help me! Help me! Help me!*

Somehow the Man knew what Ahaz was screaming in his heart, even though the spirits were screaming through his mouth, "What do want with us, Son of the Most High God?

Have You come to torment us before the appointed time?"

The face of Jesus grew hard with a warrior's fierceness. Speaking with sharp authority, He ordered the demons to leave. They screamed again, desperate to keep their place in Ahaz. "What is your name?" Jesus demanded.

The words came out of Ahaz's mouth in a tortured, anguished torrent: "Our name is Legion. . .for we are many."

"Leave him—loose him! Go to the place to await your judgment."

NOOOO! Not the abyss! Not there! Suddenly Legion noticed a herd of pigs nearby, unclean animals, but better than the abyss. "The pigs. . .the pigs. . .let us go to the pigs!"

Jesus spoke one more word: "Go!"

The spirits rushed out into the swine and sent them squealing over a cliff into the sea. A moment later two thousand pigs floated dead in the water—and nearly seven thousand demons writhed in the darkness of the abyss, bound until they would meet Jesus one final time in judgment.

Ahaz felt a great ripping sensation in his mind and body. . . and then peace. His breath, which had been coming out in rasping gasps, slowed. The dark, crazed look in his eyes disappeared. The sparkle of sanity returned. For the first time Ahaz clearly saw the Man in front of him. The face of Jesus, so fierce in spiritual battle only a moment

A legion was a military division of nearly seven thousand troops. The number suggests the number of demons inhabiting the man, and it also implies a demonic hierarchy. These spirits were under the control of other demons of higher rank, much like a human army. The Jews believed unclean spirits lived in dark, dirty places or in animals.

before, now shone with forgiving, liberating grace. Light flood-ed Ahaz's dark heart. The voices were gone. Ahaz was free!

Ahaz stared at Jesus as he realized his long dark night was over. Someone handed him a robe, and he put on clothes for the first time in months. At last he was not only in his right mind, he was also in right relationship with God. He would never be the same; Jesus had brought him freedom. Ahaz would go anywhere and everywhere Jesus went for the rest of his life.

The hog herders rushed into the village and told the en-tire town that a supernatural event had occurred. Soon the entire community streamed out to see if the herders' words were true. What they saw left them open-mouthed with amazement. Ahaz the demonized sat clothed, sane, and delivered at the feet of Jesus. Over two thousand pigs floated dead in the Sea of Galilee.

The financial implications of Ahaz's spiritual liberation were staggering. Two thousand pigs were worth a fortune. "If it costs this much for one man to be free, it costs too much," a city leader said flatly. The townspeople agreed: If Jesus' presence meant such radical changes, then Jesus would have to go.

They asked Him to leave.

Ahaz looked up in puzzled amazement when he heard the city leaders request Jesus to remove Himself from their region. What? This Man had done for him what no one else could. No matter what anyone else said, Ahaz declared that he would fol-low Jesus. He owed Jesus his life.

Jesus knelt next to His new disciple. Looking into Ahaz's eyes, Jesus said gently, "Go home to your family and friends now. Tell them the great things God has done for you." He smiled. "The best way for you to serve Me is to go back home now and rebuild the relationships you ruined. True freedom gives us the power to serve others in love."

Ahaz nodded slowly, his face shining. "Yes," he whispered. What Jesus said made perfect sense.

But then, everything Jesus does is perfect.

BEYOND THE STORY
*Questions to Nudge Your Thinking
and Nourish Your Heart*

1. The concept of personal evil spiritual forces—demons—
   that can actually influence human behavior is difficult for
   many people to accept. Many don't want to acknowledge
   things beyond their understanding or control. Think a
   moment about your beliefs in this area. What shapes those
   beliefs? If you have never found out what Scripture teaches
   about this, take time to base your beliefs in God's truth.

2. What lessons did you learn from Ahaz's downward spiritual slide? Are there any areas that need attention in your
   spiritual life?

3. What insights impress you about Ahaz after Jesus set him
   free? Christ's freedom affected many dimensions of Ahaz's
   life. List as many as you can. . .and celebrate a Savior that
   set us free in every way!

Meeting Grace

They had danced all night.

The dance was a once-a-year, all-night celebration. Now that the Illumination of the Temple was over, people went back to their daily routine. For most of them, this would be their only chance to be part of a dance of joy. As the crowd returned home, each heart secretly wished he or she could dance in the light; each one yearned to have his or her own celebration of joy, lit from within.

The next morning the air was still cool as the sun peeked above the eastern wall of the Temple. The tall columns cast long shadows into the courtyard as people streamed through the gate and began to fill the large area. Men and women talked together in low but animated voices, for this was the outer Court of the Women, where both sexes could go.

"Did you hear who is teaching this morning? It's the Carpenter from Nazareth."

"I've heard Him before, and I've not been the same since. He makes the Word of God come alive."

"Yes, they say He teaches with authority and power, not like the dry instruction of the Pharisees. They may know the Word with their heads, but they sure don't seem to know it in their hearts. Here He comes now."

All eyes in the courtyard turned to watch the entrance of the Teacher from Nazareth. He was wearing ordinary clothes, not like the fancy robes and tassels of the Pharisees. The Pharisees were "the keepers of the Law," and they dressed so people would recognize their importance, but Jesus looked like any common person. His hands showed the calluses from years at the carpenter's bench, and His arms were well muscled. His

Each year on the first night of the Feast of the Tabernacles, the four great golden candelabras in the Temple were lit as darkness descended. Fed by large bowls filled with oil, the candles burned all night, and their light was so bright that all of Jerusalem glowed. Around these candelabras those considered to be the wisest, greatest, and holiest men in all Israel danced, singing songs of joy to celebrate God's victory over the darkness of sin and His enemies. Only a select few could dance in the light. The rest, as strict Temple rules dictated, were only allowed to watch. They were not allowed to participate in the dance of joy. Finally, as night's blackness faded into the gray of day, the oil feeding the candles would run out, and the flames would flicker out.

face was open and friendly as He moved to the seat reserved for the teacher of the day.

Standing to face the expectant throng, His face broke out into a smile, and it seemed to reach out and cheer every heart. "Greetings, and the Lord's blessing be on you!" He said and sat down.

He took the scroll someone handed Him. He read from the Word of God with the familiarity of someone who loved the truth He was reading. Leaning forward, He began to apply God's Word to their lives. He used homespun stories from everyday life to transform deep spiritual themes into practical realities. His voice was strong but easy, and what He said got under the skin, right down to the heart. You couldn't listen to Him for very long and stay the same person.

Suddenly, Christ stopped speaking, His gaze looking out over the heads of the crowd to the entrance of the court. A group of men, dressed in the dark robes and tassels that identified them as Pharisees, was half-dragging and half-pushing a woman into the court. She was dressed in the light linen tunic that normally served as an undergarment beneath a woman's robe. The tunic was dirty where the woman had been dragged down the streets, and it was torn in a couple places. Strong hands held her arms in a viselike grip that made her wince and cry out. Her face was smudged, her elbows scraped from the cobblestones. The men shoved people aside, marching in silent anger as an aisle formed through the crowd to where Jesus sat. Reaching Him, they threw the woman at His feet; she landed in a crumpled heap, shivering and crying, broken and terrified. Then they jerked her upright again and made her stand before Jesus, a prisoner already found guilty.

The group of men broke into a bitter chorus of accusations, their words like blasts from a furnace, spewing out vile names for women like her, women caught in the very act of adultery. No one said how they had caught her in bed with a man who was not her husband. No man stood beside her to share the blame. No one bothered to reveal any of those important details. They had already condemned her to die.

They fingered the sharp rocks in their hands with malicious anticipation. The self-righteous glint in their eyes and their strident voices made the woman's fate a foregone conclusion.

But she was not the one who was on trial here.

Jesus was.

"Teacher, this woman was caught in the act of adultery. The law of Moses commands us to stone such a woman. What do *you* say?"

There it was. A cleverly contrived trap. If Jesus told them to let the woman go, He would be guilty of not upholding the Jewish law—and He would be branded a heretic. If He consented to the stoning of the woman, He would be in violation of Roman law, which forbade public executions outside Roman jurisdiction. Either way, Jesus would be discredited and His ministry seriously undermined. The Pharisees waited, undisguised triumph on their faces, like wolves ready for the kill.

Jesus sat still for a long moment, looking steadily into the eyes of each of the men, one at a time. No fear or apprehension showed in His face. He seemed to be looking straight into each man, as if seeing past the exterior appearance to the inner man. Then Jesus bent down and began to write in the sand with His finger.

After a minute He looked up again and said, slowly and distinctly, "If any one of you is without sin, let him be the first to throw a stone at her." He leaned down and began to write again.

Letter by letter, the word took shape: EXTORTIONER. Jesus looked up and met the eyes of the group's leader. The man's face paled, and his eyes bulged with stark terror. The rock dropped from his hand and he was gone, slipping into the shadows at the back of the crowd.

Jesus' keen gaze rested one by one on the woman's accusers. Then He wrote again in the sand at their feet, word after word. The Pharisees watched His finger in horrified fascination, as it traveled up and down, up and down. They could not watch without trembling. They thought of the finger of God writing on the wall in the time of Daniel, revealing His judgment. They had howled for justice. Now it had descended on them. As He looked into their faces, Jesus saw into their very hearts, and His moving finger wrote on. . .

Idolater. . .

Liar. . .

Drunk. . .

Murderer. . .

Adulterer. . .

Dull thuds echoed off the columns as stone after stone fell on the pavement. One by one, the self-appointed prosecutors slunk off into the shadows, leaving the woman standing alone, surrounded by the stones that would have brought her death. No one had been qualified to cast the first stone.

The woman's quiet sobbing broke the stillness. She had still not raised her head. Kneeling in front of her, Jesus lifted her chin to meet His eyes, and for a long moment neither of them spoke.

As she looked into the face of Christ, a thought sprang into her mind: *He could have thrown the first stone!* She was guilty, of that there was no question—but He was guiltless, and yet He had not carried out the death sentence she deserved. Instead of being afraid, she found her heart broken with sorrow for her sin. All her excuses fell away. She looked up at Jesus with pain in her eyes, her fate in His hands.

Jesus saw in her gaze her acceptance of her guilt. He saw her deep pain and her longing to be free from the prison in which her own conscience had locked her. His eyes, so strong and piercing, grew soft with compassion.

In his face she saw the force of God's holiness upholding His law—but she saw something else as well. Something she had never seen before. . .kindness. . .no, something deeper than that.

It was mercy mixed with love. . .

It was grace.

With eyes full of understanding, Jesus said, "Woman, where are your accusers? Has no one condemned you?"

"No man, Lord." She did not call Him Teacher or Sir, but Lord. She had yielded her life to Him.

Jesus answered softly, yet loud enough so the onlooking crowd, spellbound by the human drama unfolding before them, could hear clearly. "Then neither do I condemn you. Go and leave your life of sin."

Deep within her heart, the woman changed. Her sin had not been excused. He had not ignored the terrible thing she had done. He could have cast the first stone, but He had not. He could have condemned her and been entirely justified in doing so, but He did not. Instead, He went beyond the demands of the Law and chose instead to forgive. Her old life died within her, and a new life began. In her spirit, she was clean, like a newborn baby.

With eyes shining with gratitude, the woman brushed the hair from her eyes and turned to leave. Head up, she walked through the crowd toward home. She walked in the sunlight. She would need the shadows no more.

Through the entire drama the crowd sat spellbound. They had never seen anything like this. "Those religious men," they whispered to each other, "some of them even took part in the celebration last night." "Such darkness in their eyes! They were so ready to condemn, so eager to hurt." "I've never seen someone like Jesus." "He was so fearless. . .even though the Pharisees were so self-righteous." "He was so wise. . .the Pharisees were really attacking Him." "He was so kind and gracious to the guilty woman." "So willing to forgive and yet not leave her in her sin."

Forgive? A light dawned in minds throughout the great throng. To do what Jesus had just done was not possible.

Forgiveness was something only God had the authority to do.

If Jesus forgave the woman, then He would have to be. . .

Jesus had been watching the crowd. He stepped forward now, the great candelabras behind Him, their candles now darkened, and His voice rang out with invitation: "I am the light of the world! Anyone who follows Me will never walk in darkness again, but will have the light of life."

Heads nodded all across the courtyard as the light of truth broke through. Understanding filled their hearts, and their wills embraced the truth. The candles could only burn so long before going dark. Their religion, which limited closeness to God to a select few, hindered them from knowing the light of true joy.

But Jesus. . .Jesus the Christ, the Son of God, was inviting all of them to find their light in Him. They would know the joy of a real relationship with God. . .and dancing in the light would become a constant reality rather than a once-a-year spectator event. Life from God ignited hearts all over the courtyard.

Many generations have come and gone since that Jerusalem morning. Religious rituals have changed over the course of time. . .but the condition of human hearts is still the same. Pride still wears the vestments of rigid legalism. Too many people still see "church" as a place of condemnation where their sins are only talked about in terms of accusation—or excused with another kind of cultural accommodation. Either way, there's something missing. . . .

No, Someone's missing.

Only Jesus brings grace.

He doesn't throw the first stone. Instead He took the first and final blows for our sins that we rightfully deserve to bear. He bears our sin and His grace redeems us from its power.

That's what happened to a nameless woman who was caught in the dark but wound up walking free in the Light. That's what can happen to us. . .

when we come to the Light. . .

when we meet Grace.

BEYOND THE STORY
*Questions to Nudge Your Thinking
and Nourish Your Heart*

1. How do you see "church?" Many people have wanted to give up on "church" but not on God. What are some ways to bridge that gap for people?

2. As you watched Jesus respond with grace to the woman, what lessons did you "see" that will help you with your relationships with other people?

3. Where do you need grace right now in your life? What changes will happen in your life as a result of God's grace at work in you?

4. Have you "danced in the light of grace" lately? If not, take time now to celebrate the grace of Jesus—we aren't just spectators, we are participants!

Twelve
Unlikely Men

To: The Most Excellent Caiaphas, High Priest of the Temple, Spiritual Leader of Israel

Greetings in the name of the Most High. May His smile be upon you and all who worship in the Temple there in Jerusalem today.

Thank you again for choosing me for this important assignment. I know your choice was in part because I am from the north of Israel and therefore unknown, but your confidence in me as a loyal Pharisee and servant to the Sanhedrin humbles me nonetheless. I trust this report will be helpful as you and the leaders of the Sanhedrin seek to rule our nation wisely. I agree with your statement that we must protect our nation from false teaching and false religious leaders at all costs.

As I begin this report, let me summarize the assignment you gave me: For a period of time we have been hearing reports about a carpenter-turned-itinerant-teacher, one Jesus bar Joseph of Nazareth. Most of his activity has been in the region of Galilee, but reports of his teaching and supposed miracles are spreading throughout our land. You have specifically asked me to report on the followers of Jesus, especially the inner group of twelve men closest to him.

You are wise to seek to understand who they are and why Jesus may have chosen them. I have been following Jesus and this group of twelve at length now, watching them in many situations. Most of them I have engaged in conversation at different times, or I have talked to those who know them well. Sometimes I have talked to them about each other, seeking to find out why they continue to follow this Nazarene carpenter. I have been somewhat surprised to find how open they are to talking with me. They seem eager to tell their stories to all who will hear, but most of all they love to talk about Jesus of Nazareth.

I will give a brief report on each of the twelve, but let me say

> Galilee is north of Jerusalem, which was the cultural, political, and spiritual center of the nation. People from "up north" in Galilee were considered "lower class" by the big-city inhabitants of Jerusalem.

at the outset that these are twelve unlikely men to be considered leaders of a new religious group. None of them have the formal education we have as Pharisees, only the scant education they received from their local synagogue rabbis. Their leader has no formal education either, which means none of them are properly trained to teach the Holy Word. Almost all of them are fairly young, with two barely past their teen years. All but one come from the region of Galilee; it goes without saying that they are unsophisticated and backward compared to those from the great centers of culture, business, government, and religion. Several of them are related. Five are fishermen. These are unschooled, untrained, ordinary men. Nothing about them would make truly trained spiritual leaders give them a second look. Yet, for some reason Jesus has chosen them as his apprentices. As I describe them to you, Most Excellent Caiaphas, I believe you will agree that these men, especially apart from their leader, are among the most unqualified candidates for religious ministry I have ever seen.

The unofficial spokesman for the twelve is a fisherman from Capernaum named Simon. Jesus has given him the name "Peter," suggesting he has a rock-solid character, but he exhibits more of the qualities of shifting sand. His personality makes him appear larger than he really is. He tends to speak first and think later, leading him to appear arrogantly brash one moment and a humiliated child the next. He is impulsive, blustery, dominating, intense, often unthinking. Ruled by his emotions, this man is a study in contradictions: At times he is brave and at other times a coward; at times he appears wise and other times very foolish; at times he declares his undying faith in Jesus and at others he struggles to trust what Jesus is saying and doing.

This man is definitely too unstable to be considered a good leader, much less a rabbi. I believe if we put enough pressure on him at the right moment, he would even deny knowing Jesus.

The second of the twelve is Simon's brother, Andrew. The two were born in Bethsaida and raised there until they moved to Capernaum to become fishing partners with the two sons of Zebedee whom I will describe later in this report. Andrew is younger than Peter, and he appears smaller than he really is, mainly because he is living in the shadow of his older brother. Andrew was first a disciple of the radical "prophet" John, who some have called "the Baptizer."

Everything Peter is, Andrew is not. He is quiet, steady, does not seek to be noticed by others; you would not notice him in a crowd, where Simon would change the atmosphere in any group he entered. I do notice, however, one defining quality to this "invisible fisherman"—he always seems to be bringing someone to meet Jesus. In fact, he brought his own brother. Another time I watched him lead a small boy to meet Jesus just before a meal to five thousand men and their families. Recently I saw Andrew introduce some Greeks to Jesus. Although Andrew's quiet enthusiasm may influence individuals, he demonstrates no capabilities for leading groups. Andrew of Capernaum is probably only included among the twelve because of his brother.

The third of the twelve is James, son of Zebedee of Capernaum, of a priestly and royal line. He is the older brother of John, who is also among the twelve. They are also from nearby Bethsaida, and true to the meaning of the town's name, they still carry the lingering scent of a "fishhouse." With Simon,

James is the head of a successful fishing enterprise. He is a shrewd, ambitious businessman, a quality that he appears to have inherited from his father. . .and his mother. Apparently, she is the "neck that turns the head" in this family. I have even watched her push Jesus to grant her two sons more authority within their small group, trying to capitalize on the fact that she is the sister of Jesus' mother. Such brashness clearly runs in this family. James is strong, willful, self-righteous, and quick to become angry; Jesus has even given him and his brother the nickname "Sons of Thunder." Although James is a man of action and a leader in his business, his temper and inflexibility make him unsuitable for religious service.

The fourth of the twelve is John, the brother of James. He is much younger than his older brother, and although he is prone to the same outbursts of anger as his brother, he has a more sensitive temperament. He also followed John "the Baptizer" until turning his allegiance to the Nazarene. He is good friends with Andrew, both of them young men who live in the shadows of older, more aggressive brothers. He is probably the most intense of Jesus' followers, wanting to be close to his teacher all the time. He seems to drink in the words of Jesus, as if he is storing them away to write them down at a later time. Where James is a man of big actions, John appears to be a man of deep thoughts, as if he is trying to understand a bigger picture as he follows the Nazarene. However, his youth, lack of experience, unstable emotions, and meddling mother would disqualify him from any serious service.

The fifth of the twelve comes from a class of people we would not even allow in our Temple: despised tax collectors paid by Rome. This man's place of business is in Capernaum.

He is the son of Alphaeus, brother to another one of the twelve they have called "James the Less," and his name is Levi—but he does not live up to a name given to a tribe of priests.

As you know, Most Excellent Caiaphas, tax collectors are known for being dishonest and greedy, making money off the heavy tax burden Rome has laid on our backs. This Levi is a traitor, an agent of the enemy, a licensed thief. No respectable person would even have this man as a guest in his house, nor could he even testify in court. He uses his natural abilities—a keen, orderly mind and a propensity for numbers—along with more education than most from his area to serve the idol of money under the shield of Roman law. His whole lifestyle is repulsive to me; I have found it difficult to even speak to him. Yet, Jesus invited this man to follow him, and Levi has left his tax gathering for the teachings of the Nazarene. Jesus has given him the wholly inappropriate name "Matthew"— gift of God. Apparently, Levi is related to Jesus, a cousin, which may be part of the reason why he was invited to be a disciple. His considerable financial means may also be a factor.

It would be bad enough if Jesus had invited only one publican to follow him, but "Matthew" has made Jesus the guest of honor at several parties for others of his unwanted class. The Nazarene actually seems to enjoy these people. Still, the Nazarene's choice of a man like this is puzzling. We would never even let him near our doors.

The sixth of the twelve is Philip, probably named after the ruler of Iturea. As you know, this Philip did much to build up their little village of Bethsaida. I have heard that Philip has grown up influenced by Greek thinking, and he tries to blend the influence of Greek culture with our Jewish ways. The result is a man who is never quite sure about what to think. He is very cautious and slow to make decisions. He studies issues to the point of being paralyzed by his desire to have things all in order before he makes a commitment. He is precise to a fault. I am surprised Jesus would choose a man like this, but in fact, Jesus actually sought Philip out as one of his followers. A man of Philip's mindset would have never taken the initiative to make such a decision himself. However, he is somewhat responsible for bringing another of the twelve to Jesus, a man named Nathaniel. Philip's invitation was less than a ringing endorsement, however, since all Philip could tell Nathaniel when he asked about Jesus was "come and see." A man of such indecisiveness certainly would not qualify for any position of influence.

The seventh of the twelve is Philip's friend Nathaniel. He is also called Bartholomew, son of Tolmai from Cana of Galilee. He is quite different from Philip, so mystical that he is usually impractical. He loves to have his nose in scrolls, studying and meditating, and he fancies himself a student of prophecy. Actually, he is little more than a self-educated man, and he is so spiritually minded that he is almost childlike. In fact, Jesus said of him, "Here is a man in whom there is no guile." This is the kind of man who could never survive the difficult arena of religious politics. He would be unreliable because he would always be lost in his daydreams. No, he is wholly unsuitable for any kind of religious leadership.

(As you may have noticed, Most Excellent Caiaphas, the Nazarene appears to have no rhyme or reason in regard to his choices for his inner circle of twelve. As I describe the rest of the twelve, you will see even more plainly the foolishness of his choices.)

The eighth of the twelve is Simon from Canaan, a member of the Zealots. You know how this radical group has made life difficult for us in many ways. Their self-professed love for our nation has led to so many terroristic acts of violence that our entire land lives in anxiety because of them. Their obsession for restoring their version of divine rule to our land makes it difficult for us to try to accommodate the Roman situation. Their love of country is destroying the country we love.

Simon is like so many Zealots: intense, passionate, hot-blooded, highly opinionated. Maybe Jesus chose him because of his passion, but putting a tax-hating Zealot and a tax-collecting Roman hireling on the same team is puzzling at best and stupid at worst. Still, I have been surprised to see these two opposites work together under the Nazarene's direction. They still have intense discussions at times, but they appear to have put aside their opinions for the sake of following Jesus. However, such a radical, fanatical person as this Simon cannot be a good candidate for religious power.

The ninth of the twelve is another fisherman named Thomas of Galilee. He is nicknamed "Didymus"—the twin—but his twin is not among the twelve. If I were Jesus, I would be glad

Zealots were intense patriots that used religion as part of their doctrine. However, violence and murder were acceptable means to their end, especially against those considered their enemies. Their enemies included the hated Roman occupying army and anyone they felt collaborated with the Romans. After a rebellion led by famous Zealot, Judah of Gamala, twenty-five years before Jesus began His ministry, their motto became "No God but Jehovah, no tax but the Temple, no friend but a Zealot."

his twin is not part of the group, because this Thomas is a con-
tinual cloud on them. If the twins have matching personalities,
the group certainly doesn't need two such pessimis-tic, skeptical,
moody, stubborn, fatalistic brooders. Thomas always seems to be
questioning things and doubts even the most obvious realities.
He is just stubborn enough to follow the Nazarene anywhere he
goes, but his depressing attitude makes me wonder how Jesus
puts up with him. I would not have the patience.

The tenth of the twelve is another man named James, this
one the son of Alphaeus. He, too, is from Capernaum, and he
is quite different from his brother Levi, whom Jesus calls
"Matthew." James resembles the Nazarene in appearance so
much that some people mistake James for Jesus, but his contri-
bution to the group appears to be minimal. I have yet to see
him stand out in any way. If you or I were making the choice,
we would want someone more visibly productive.

The eleventh is a man known by three names. Depending
on whom you talk to, he is known as Lebbaeus, Thaddeus, or
Judas, son of James. He has a lively and active temperament,
but is also very young; he is the grandson of Zebedee and the
son of James the fisherman. He, too, has not distinguished
himself in any way, and I know no reason why he should be
considered for religious leadership.

The twelfth is the only one not from the region of Galilee.
His name is Judas from Kerioth in Judea, and they call him Judas
Iscariot to distinguish him from the other Judas. He appears to be
somewhat uneasy with the differences in language, customs, and
tradition of the Galileans in Jesus' group. He is from the tribe of
Judah, and he has some good organizational skills; in fact, the
Nazarene has made him the keeper of their purse.

There is something about the way he handles their money however, that has made me take notice, the way he almost caresses the money bag when he thinks no one else is looking. I suspect he has been embezzling funds from the group. He appears to be a man of double mind and motive, and I believe we could use this to our advantage. He could be turned against Jesus for the right price. In fact, of all the followers of Jesus, Judas Iscariot is probably the only man I might consider as a potential part of our group.

As you can see, Most Excellent Caiaphas, these men do not have the character, the credentials, nor the credibility for a cohesive religious team. The only one among them that poses any threat to us is Jesus himself. If he were taken out of the picture, his little flock would scatter and never be heard from again. I am beginning to understand why you feel it may be good for one man to die for the good of the nation. Following Jesus has indeed changed these men's lives, but the only way this little band of twelve could be any threat to us would be if Jesus somehow put his spirit into them.

Thus ends my written report, Most Excellent Caiaphas. I will gladly tell you more in person when I see you again in Jerusalem. I am glad this assignment is coming to a close, because I was uneasy being with these people. I certainly could never see myself being a part of a group such as this.

Until I see you in person, may the blessings of the Almighty surround you.

Shalom,
Saul of Tarsus

BEYOND THE STORY
*Questions to Nudge Your Thinking
and Nourish Your Heart*

1. As you reviewed the "qualifications" for spiritual leadership through the eyes of Saul (later known as the Apostle Paul), what did you notice? Now read Mark 3:13–19. What differences do you see as you watch Jesus choose His disciples?

2. What did you see about the differences in age, education, personality, and family backgrounds among the twelve Jesus chose? How does this affect your view of being a follower of Jesus?

3. *"When they saw the courage of Peter and John and realized that they were unschooled, ordinary men, they were astonished and they took note that these men had been with Jesus"* (Acts 4:13). What has this story taught you about the true nature of discipleship? Have you been allowing anything in your life to hinder you from being a wholehearted follower of Jesus? If so, let go of those hindrances now. Step out and follow in His steps.

4. Saul of Tarsus, who fought vehemently against the followers of Christ, later became one of the greatest Christian leaders in history. How can this historical fact help you as you love people who appear stubbornly resistant to Jesus at this point in their lives?

The Touch
of Faith

She drew her shawl around her thin shoulders, shivering, even though the day was sunny and warm. Constantly chilled, her body tried to fight off a fever but was never quite able to do it. Both fever and chills were only symptoms of something far more serious.

For twelve long years she had battled her sickness, a bleeding cancer that slowly drained her life. Still young, her body looked and felt a hundred years old. She was tired, so very tired. Her disease had changed her physically, emotionally, and spiritually.

Physically, her bony limbs, gray complexion, and dark, sunken eyes told the story to all who looked at her. The bleeding was noticeable and smelly, debilitating and embarrassing. She was ashamed. She had not looked anyone in the eye for twelve years.

Oh, she had been to doctors, lots of them. They had poked and prodded, given her remedies to try. She smiled grimly as she remembered all the prescriptions she had endured, ranging from the painfully astringent to the puzzlingly superstitious. In fact, the Talmud gave at least eleven cures for her physical dilemma.

One writer, Rabbi Jochanan, wrote, "Take of the gum Alexandria, and of crocus hortensis, the weight of a zuzee each, let them be bruised together, and given in wine to the woman that has an issue of blood. But if this fail, take of Persian onions nine logs, boil them in wine, and give it to her to drink: and say, Arise from your flux. But should this fail, set her in a place where two ways meet, and let her hold a cup of wine in her hand: and let someone come behind and frighten her, and say, Arise from your flux. But should this do no good, take a handful of cummin and a handful of crocus and a handful of faenu-greek; let these be boiled, and given her to drink and say to her, Arise from your flux. But should this also fail, dig seven trenches and burn in them some cuttings of vines not yet circumcised—not yet four years old—and let her take in her hand a cup of wine, and let her be led from this trench and set down over that, and let her be removed from that, and set down over another, and in each removal say to her, Arise from your flux."

All of them had failed. She had even tried some of the most bizarre "cures" anyone sane and sober could imagine. She had tried carrying the ashes of an ostrich egg in a linen rag in the summer and a cotton rag in the winter. She had even picked out and carried a barley corn she retrieved from the dung of a white she-donkey. All those attempts at healing. . .all those desperate efforts at physical recovery. . .and none of them had worked. She had steadily grown worse. The only thing of which the doctors had relieved her was her money. When she had nothing left to pay, they had told her that her disease was incurable. Now poverty was added to the weight of pain she woke up to every day.

Emotionally, the disease had drained her as well. According to the Law, she was "unclean." That meant no one was allowed to touch her or come in contact with her without the risk of becoming "unclean" as well. No one was willing to take that risk. For twelve years she had lived without the strength of close friendship. No hug encouraged her in times of discouragement, no caring hand touched her gently when the suffering was too hard to bear.

Spiritually, she was ready to give up hope. At first she had prayed and pleaded with God to help her. Even though she had never been very religious before, when suffering came she had instinctively looked up to a God who seemed distant and unknowable. Somehow she knew her only hope was in Him, yet she didn't know how to reach Him and let Him touch her life. She had tried to worship in the Temple, thinking she might find Him there, but the priests turned her away because she was "unclean." She faced each day with loneliness, pain, and hopelessness as her only companions. They were the only ones who stayed with her. Society had ostracized her, her own body had turned against her, even God seemed to have abandoned her. Every sunset was stained with the blood of her pain. She was an orphan. Abandoned. Alone.

One day as she looked outside the window of her tiny

dwelling, she saw someone she recognized, a man who had been "unclean" like herself. He was a leper, a fellow outcast—but something was different about him now. He walked upright with a spring in his step she had not seen before. Then she noticed his skin—it was healthy and suntanned, not white and spotted as before. He seemed to be an entirely new man. Noticing her, he walked over to her windowsill and began to tell her what had happened.

Just a few days ago, he said, he had been sitting along the road when a crowd of people approached. At the center of the crowd's attention was a Man. He was rather common in appearance, His hands callused, as if from manual labor, His smiling face suntanned. Yet, there was something different about Him, something the leper could not describe. . .something, well, kingly about Him.

Then the leper heard the Man's name from the people who were walking with Him: Jesus. This was the Carpenter from Nazareth everyone was talking about. The One who was traveling about the hills and villages of the countryside, teaching and healing.

The One they were calling the Son of God.

For the sick man, this was a chance he had to take, an opportunity he might never get again. The crowd parted to make room for him, and he made an earnest, simple request: "Lord, if You are willing, You can make me clean."

Jesus' answer was just as simple, and His smile disarmed the leper's fears and sparked his hope. "If I'm willing! Friend, all things are possible to him who believes." And with that, Jesus reached out and touched the untouchable man. That touch healed him.

"Jesus healed me," he said now to the sick woman. "Maybe He can heal you, too. He's still in our area, near the town square. Why don't you go see for yourself?" With that, the former leper went on his way, whistling.

She sat thinking a long time. Her hopes had been raised and then crushed too many times. Why should this Carpenter-Teacher-Healer be any different? Should she risk being disappointed again? She had prayed before, and nothing had seemed to happen. God had been so far away.

Yet if they were calling this Man the Son of God, then she could get close to God. Maybe this time would be different.

She had come to the most important point of her life: the end of herself and her resources. She could discard her faith now and give up forever—or she could get up and direct her faith to the One who had healed the leper.

With a new look of determination in her eyes, a look that had not been there for years, she got up from her chair. She would see this Jesus. She had no money to pay Him, no reason for Him to want to help her, and yet she slowly willed her frail body toward the town square.

As she neared the center of the village, she heard the sound of many voices. The crowd was eager, happy, buzzing with excited energy. As she came around the corner of a building, she saw a man push his way into the heart of the crowd, a look of pain and desperation on his face, and she recognized Jairus, one of the religious leaders. He fell on his knees in front of a Man at the center of the teeming mass of people.

The Man was dressed in the common garb of a rabbi— open-toed sandals, a seamless inner garment fastened with a braided cloth belt, covered by an outer robe. The robe, called a tallith, had white thread fringes on the four corners. His head was covered with a maaphoeth, a linen towel that descended to His shoulders, kept in place with a braided headband. The woman's heart told her she was looking at the Man who held the key to the lock of her illness.

The buzzing crowd grew silent as it watched a leading citizen humble himself in front of Jesus, tears streaming down his face. Jairus poured out the story of a sick daughter, only twelve years old, near to death. "All the doctors have given up hope. Can You possibly do anything?" Looking at the helpless father, deep compassion in His eyes, Jesus put His hand on Jairus's shoulder and agreed to go to his home. Jairus leapt to his feet, nodding eagerly. There was not a moment to lose.

The woman's heart sank. Jairus had standing and influence in the community; she was a nobody. He was religious, while there was nothing about her that deserved help, only her desperate condition. The thought sprang into her mind that she had lived with her plight as long as Jairus's daughter had been alive. Eyes haunted by hope lost, she knew her chance had flown away. She turned disconsolately to head back to her home.

But the crowd turned down her street! Maybe she would have a chance to meet Jesus after all. . .maybe. . .maybe if she could just touch the hem or even the fringe of His robe, that would be enough. No one would notice her, and Jesus could continue on His way to the sick girl's home. She could snatch a miracle from Jesus without Him noticing it.

While these thoughts ran through her mind, she was suddenly swept up in the eager crowd. She found herself behind Jesus, only feet away but separated by what seemed like miles of densely packed humanity.

If I can only touch the border of His robe. . . . I must touch Him, I must get some of His power. . . .

She tried to push her way though the crowd, struggling against the teeming throng. Nearer and nearer. . .one step closer. . . . Her breath came in ragged gasps; her ribs ached from the exertion and the sharp elbows that jabbed her sides.

She stumbled as someone pushed in front of her. *No!* He must not pass so near and yet so far away. She could not bear to lose this last chance. Her strength fading quickly, a low moan escaped her lips; panicked, she surged forward, reaching. . . straining. . . Just a little farther. . . Now she could almost reach Him. . . . He seemed to hesitate at that moment. She stumbled again and fell to her knees—but with the tip of one finger she touched His robe.

That was enough! With a surge of warmth, life poured back into her body. Shrunken veins coursed with vibrant liquid strength; withered limbs filled out with new muscle; skin gray and pallid with sickness suddenly turned pink with health. She breathed deeply without pain for the first time in a dozen years. . .and she knew she was whole. She slipped back into the crowd, unnoticed. . .she thought. No one noticed her. . . no one but Christ!

Jesus stopped and turned around, as if looking for someone. "Who touched My robe?"

One of the men near Him, apparently a disciple of His, looked at Jesus in amazement. "You see all these people crowding around You, and yet You ask who touched You?"

Jesus shook his head slightly as He continued to look around Him. "Someone touched Me. I can tell that power has gone out from Me to someone." Dozens of puzzled faces turned toward

Jesus. He scanned each face until His eyes met the woman's.

He knew! She waited for Jesus to point an accusing finger at her. Instead, He reached out His hand and beckoned for her to come closer. Trembling with fear, she came and fell at His feet, pouring out her whole story: the years of pain, the loneliness, the lack of human help. She opened her heart completely to Him, and then, having confessed it all, she waited for His response.

A silence fell across the crowd, and for a long moment all attention focused on the Christ and the woman who trembled at His feet.

Jesus reached down and took the woman by the hand, helping her to her feet. With His other hand He gently lifted her chin until her eyes met His. His own eyes were moist, and she knew He understood her suffering. Softly, but for all to hear, He said, "Daughter, your faith has healed you. Go in peace and be freed from your suffering."

Daughter. He had called her daughter! Her heart suddenly told her that Jesus had done more than merely heal her body; He had made her spiritually whole as well. She was part of God's family now. The sickness that separated her from others was gone. She was a new woman, with a new body and a new heart. Her eyes bright with joy, she nodded her head in understanding and thanks. Jesus turned again to head for the home of Jairus; she walked down the street, unashamed and secure.

Like a nameless woman many generations ago, we, too, can reach out and touch Jesus. We may feel we have little strength and feeble faith, but that is not what matters. What matters is not the size of our faith, but the power of our Healer. Jesus

Christ brings us healing in ways we don't always understand. Real faith does not demand or direct how healing should be accomplished, it only touches Jesus with complete confidence, trusting Him with the details.

If you've been living in the dark night of despair, reach out in simple faith. Jesus sees you in the crowd. He knows your heart. He knows your need.

Touch Him, and watch His power flood your life.

BEYOND THE STORY
*Questions to Nudge Your Thinking
and Nourish Your Heart*

1. Long-term disappointment is a drain emotionally, physically, and spiritually to many people's lives. Are you or someone you know living with a situation like this? How are your feelings similar to or different from the experience of the woman in this story?

2. Many people think faith is only agreeing with a set of beliefs. When life's circumstances don't match what our head tells us, it can be easy to feel God has let us down or our faith must be wrong. The nameless woman in this story went past what her head told her and acted with her heart. What does that teach you about faith?

3. It's not the size of our faith but the size of our Healer that makes the difference. Faith is more than words, it is action. It is cooperating with the promises and power of God. How can that change the way you are praying about some situations in your life right now?

4. Many are like those who could have reached out to the woman—afraid to get involved with a difficult, draining situation in someone else's life. Jesus said, "Whatever you did for one of the least of these brothers of mine, you did for me." (Matthew 25:40 NIV). Find someone who desperately needs a word of encouragement, a tender touch, a listening ear. Let Jesus give you grace to share with that person. He will give grace *to* you so He can bring grace *through* you.

Lunch for 20,000

"One. . .two. . .three. . .four. . .five, six, seven. Seven skips. That's my best ever!" Jesse's seven-year-old face blossomed into an ear-to-ear grin as the ripples of the stone spread out into the Sea of Galilee.

Too bad no one was here to see it, he thought. Such important events were to be celebrated. Wait until he got home and told his older brother, Samuel. Boy, would he be jealous. Samuel might be two years older, but *he* had never skipped a stone seven times.

Samuel was already old enough to work, so he wouldn't be getting in much stone-skipping any time soon. It wouldn't be long before Jesse would be putting in full days, too. Everyone had to do his share; life was hard, and their large family was poor. Time to play was a luxury they didn't get to enjoy very often, so Jesse was going to make the most of this day at the lake.

He looked out across the water, calm and just right for rock skipping. The shore of the Sea of Galilee was covered by so many rocks that Jesse could throw stones all day and no one would notice any were missing. He'd thrown dozens already.

Rubbing his nose with the back of his hand, he looked up at the sun. . .way past noon already. No wonder he was hungry! It had been hours since his mother had packed him a small bundle for his trip to the shore. He had walked a couple miles from his home in Bethsaida up in the rocky hills down the descending path to the lake.

Life was difficult for most people in Israel. Life expectancy was only about thirty years, so children often began working very young, married young, and started their families young. Children often learned the trade of their fathers, apprenticing in a business that families carried on for generations.

Here lots of green, thick grass grew down the slope of the hill to the shore. He could throw himself down on the cushiony carpet and roll over and over down to where the grass met the pebbles on the beach. Besides that, there were rocks to skip, birds to watch as they floated over the water, bugs to catch. . .who had time to eat? Still, his stomach was beginning to growl, so he walked over to where he'd laid down his bundle.

There wasn't much in it. His mother had packed him five small flat loaves of barley bread and two small pickled fish not much longer than his little finger. That was his food for the day, so he would be careful not to eat it all at once.

They were so poor that they couldn't even afford wheat for

their bread. Barley was three times cheaper, so they only got wheat bread on very special occasions. Still, his family was rich in love, so Jesse didn't realize how difficult life really was for them. Sometimes when he lay in bed at night, he heard his father and mother talking in low tones about how to provide for their family. Often his mother's voice carried a note of worry, but Jesse's father always spoke with reassurance to her. When he heard his father talking like that, he could always close his eyes and fall asleep easily. Jesse trusted his father. There always seemed to be enough for their family, because his father worked hard and took his responsibility to provide for them seriously.

Yet, his father wasn't so serious that he couldn't have fun, too. Jesse would try to help his father most days, and sometimes as they worked together, his father would toss him over one of his broad shoulders, spinning him around until they both were dizzy and laughing. Jesse couldn't wait to be big enough to help his father all the time. When he grew up, he wanted to be just like his father.

He had just picked up his lunch bag when he heard the sound of people approaching him, the buzz of excited voices out of place here where it was normally so quiet. Jesse shielded his eyes and squinted as he looked at the approaching crowd. Wow! So many of them. A line so long he couldn't see the end stretched out along the shore from the direction of Capernaum . . .and that was nine miles away! Why would all these people be out here?

Then he saw some of them pointing out into the lake, and Jesse swung his gaze back out across the water. Out in the distance he could see a fishing boat coming toward them. The sail was up, but it was making slow time because of the slight breeze. Whoever was on that boat was attracting the attention of all these people.

Suddenly Jesse was surrounded by the first group to get to the shore, swallowed up by the men and women. They were so focused on the ship, they didn't even notice him. Several large adults jostled him as they pressed up to the water's edge. He turned and bumped his nose against the elbow of the man next to him. . .*ouch!* Sometimes being a kid was no fun. Grown-ups mostly ignored you, unless you got in the way. . .and you couldn't see good in a crowd when you were barely taller than most people's waists. At that moment Jesse was not enjoying being a kid at all.

He peered up into the face of a woman next to him. She looked worried and tired at the same time, like his mother looked sometimes when things were hard. She was gazing anxiously out across the lake.

"Do you think it's Him?" she asked no one in particular. "Yes, it has the same sail as the boat we saw leaving Capernaum. It's got to be Him." She was talking to herself like grown-ups do sometimes. Jesse caught snatches of conversation from others in the crowd, and slowly he began to piece together what was happening.

They were all waiting for a man named Jesus. Many of them were on their way to the Passover Feast in Jerusalem, but they wanted to see Jesus before going any farther. Some were wondering how Jesus felt about the recent death of John the Baptizer, who had been beheaded by Herod, the ruler of their region. Others were hoping to receive a miracle from Jesus, like others had who they had heard about. Most of the people sounded worried and weary like the lady next to him, and they all couldn't wait to see Jesus.

Jesus. Jesse had heard of the carpenter-teacher from Nazareth. Stories about Him were shared over dinner tables, in market squares, and outside synagogues all over the region. Women talked about Him to each other as they went to get water at the community well. Men debated the validity of His miracles as they paused during work. Even children whispered about Him, comparing things they heard their parents say. The number of opinions about Jesus were as varied as the stories told about Him. Jesse had wondered what He was really like. Could He really heal sick people? Did bad spirits really shriek and leave people at His command? And what about that girl that was dead until Jesus came to her house?

Jesse still clutched his lunch, but he had forgotten all about eating, caught up in the crowd's growing excitement. His attention was now completely on the fishing boat. It was almost here! He could see the faces of the men in the boat. They looked tired and none too eager to see the throng of people at the water's edge. . .all except one.

One face, also obviously very weary, didn't look at the gathering with ill-disguised irritation like the rest of the men. Instead, Jesse saw a look of tenderness come across those tired features, like he had seen one time in the face of his father when Jesse was in bed sick. His father had put his hand gently on his head and said, "If I could take the pain away from you and put it into me, I would." That was the expression on this man's face. Instinctively, Jesse knew that face belonged to Jesus.

The boat finally reached shore, and the men climbed over the sides, splashing water as they slogged ashore. A couple of them looked back at Jesus as if expecting a signal from Him to send the people away. Instead, Jesus smiled, nodding slightly toward the crowd, and motioned with His eyes to a spot up the hill from the shoreline.

With that, several disciples turned to the crowd and asked

them to make way for their group. As Jesus' helpers reached shore, the throng parted for them, forming a long winding narrow corridor of humanity. Jesse counted the men from the boat as they walked past him: one, two, three, four. . .twelve helpers in all. Last of all came Jesus. As He walked ashore, the crowd seemed to lean toward Him.

People were pushing against Jesse again, and the man with the sharp elbow bumped him. Panic seized Jesse as he felt himself falling into the water. . .but suddenly two strong arms caught him. Looking up, Jesse found himself gazing into the smiling face of Jesus.

What a face! He didn't look all that different from most other men—a dark beard, strong features sun-bronzed from much time outdoors—but there was a twinkle in those eyes that made Jesse feel he'd just found a brand-new friend. "Th–thanks, mister," Jesse managed to stammer.

Jesus tousled his hair and winked at him. "Come with Me," He said.

Jesse gulped, his eyes wide. Go with Jesus? "Sure!" His voice squeaked, but Jesus just put his arm around Jesse's little shoulders, and the two of them walked up the hill through the narrow corridor of folks. Jesus didn't seem bothered by the pressure of the crowd or their needs all around Him. Instead, He appeared to be energized from some unseen source of strength, and He reached out His free hand to people in greeting as they walked.

The human tunnel seemed like it would never end. Jesse couldn't see anything but halfway up faceless bodies as they crossed the pebbled beach, onto the carpet of grass, and up the hillside to where the twelve helpers had found a rock for Jesus to sit. When Jesus sat down, Jesse saw they were almost to the top of the hill. Below them the crowd flowed all the way down the hill, down to the water's edge. . .and the line of people from Capernaum was still coming. "Wow," Jesse whispered. He had never seen so many people at once. "There must be thousands of them."

Jesus motioned to one of his helpers, who gently led Jesse off to the side, still clutching his small bundle. "My name is Andrew," the helper said. "I'm one of Jesus' disciples. Would you like to stay with us and watch?"

Jesse looked up into Andrew's friendly face and nodded. He wouldn't miss this for anything. A day by himself at the beach had just turned into an adventure he'd talk about the rest of his life.

Jesus sat and watched the people as they came. . .and Jesse watched Jesus. He could see that Jesus was really tired. The dark circles under his eyes reminded Jesse of how his dad looked at the end of a long day. But Jesse also saw that same look of tenderness he had noticed earlier. Jesse could tell Jesus was thinking about the vast mass of people more than His own weariness.

Jesus leaned over to one of His disciples, a big, burly, balding man who looked like a fisherman. "Look at them, Peter," Jesus said. "They look like sheep. . .scared, lost, helpless, as if they had no shepherd. I know you're tired. . .but don't you think we should help them?"

Peter looked at Jesus, then out across the crowd, then back to Jesus. "Yes, Lord," he said. "You just tell us what to do. We'll help in any way we can."

Jesus nodded, satisfied with Peter's response. Standing up, Jesus raised His arms in greeting. The crowd quieted, all faces turned toward Him in eager expectation. "Welcome!" He called out. The hillside formed a natural amplification system, carrying His voice so all could hear. Thousands of voices returned

His greeting. "I have good news for you," Jesus went on in a clear strong voice. "The Kingdom of God is come—and with the King of the Universe all things are possible!" Hundreds of faces nodded in agreement, each silently urging Jesus to go on.

With that Jesus began to teach. He started by telling simple stories, painting pictures with His words that even a boy Jesse's age could easily understand. As He told the stories, Jesus showed how the things of God's creation point each person to better know God as Creator. . .and Savior. . .and Healer. . .and Father . . .and Friend. Jesse found himself hanging on every word.

This Jesus wasn't like any rabbi Jesse had heard at the synagogue; Jesse could understand Jesus. Usually Jesse felt like the rabbi was shaking his finger at him, pointing out his wrongs, promising God's punishment if he didn't do better; but as Jesus spoke, Jesse felt He was beckoning to him with His finger, inviting him to share God's love and power. The verses from the Scriptures were the same, but the tone was entirely different. The God Jesus was talking about was the kind of God Jesse wanted to know.

Before he knew it, Jesse could see by the sun that over an hour had gone by. He felt as though Jesus had just started teaching. "Now. . . ," Jesus said, "you have heard the good news of the Kingdom. But the Kingdom of God is not a matter of just words. It is God's power available to you right here, right now. If you would like God to touch your life, come and I will pray with you."

People began coming from all over, dozens, hundreds! The helpers guided them into a line, and one by one Jesus began to receive them. Some came limping on a crutch. Others were literally carried by family or friends. Some carried canes that identified them as blind to the sighted people around them. Jesse saw many parents carrying children with eyes dull and dark from fever. A few had a strange look in their eyes that made Jesse uneasy.

But Jesus treated each person with an attitude of quiet confidence. Sometimes He asked a brief question, listening closely and nodding as He looked compassionately into the eyes of the seeker. Other times He would just look with deep understanding, as if He already knew what the need was before the person even spoke. Then, gently and respectfully, Jesus would put His hand on the shoulder or the head of the man, woman, or child in front of Him and softly speak, often smiling with reassurance as He did.

What Jesse saw made his eyes wide. A man with twisted, shriveled legs carried by four others was suddenly standing on his own, shouting with amazed joy, "I can walk. . .I can walk!" A wave of cheers washed down the hillside and back up again as people turned to each other to announce the visible evidence of a miracle. One after another the miracles continued —a blind man with tears running down his face as he saw for the first time blue sky, green grass, and his Healer's face. Once-sick children ran ahead of their parents back down the hill; men and women who had the unbalanced look on their faces walked away in peaceful sanity. Everyone Jesus touched was changed.

The line was long, but Jesus continued until late-afternoon shadows began to cover them. He didn't seem to notice, but finally one of His disciples came alongside of him. Jesse leaned in close to hear what he was saying: "Master, it is late in the day. These people came without bringing any food with them. We need to send them on their way so they can reach the surrounding villages before dark and get themselves something to eat."

Jesus turned so He could face the disciple, then looked

around at all of them. "No. . .let's not. Why don't you men give them something to eat?"

Twelve puzzled faces stared back at Him. One of the disciples mentioned that they had left so quickly on the boat they didn't even have food for themselves, much less anyone else. Jesus paused for a moment, then turned to one of the twelve and gestured toward him.

"Philip, you're from around here. . .where can we go to get bread for these hungry people?" The question carried a tone that made it seem as though Jesus had asked more than just the location of the nearest bakery. Philip suddenly looked very uncomfortable, and he studied the ground at his feet, scuffing the dirt in indecision.

When he looked up, his face wore a helpless expression. "Lord. . .it would take eight months' wages just to buy enough bread to give everyone in this crowd even a bite. We don't have that kind of money. We don't even have bread for ourselves." Eleven other faces mirrored Philip's resignation. Jesus didn't say anything, but He did appear a little disappointed in Philip's response.

For a long moment no one spoke, and Jesse felt bad with the rest of them. *Boy,* he thought. *I wish there was something I could do. Wait a minute.* He still had his lunch. It wasn't much but. . .

He tugged on Andrew's sleeve. Andrew knelt down to meet him at eye level, and Jesse held out his small bundle. Andrew unwrapped it and looked inside, then back up at Jesse.

"You can have it if it will help." Jesse expected Andrew to laugh at him, but instead he just smiled and nodded a thank you.

"Come with me." Andrew brought Jesse in front of Jesus. "This boy has five barley loaves and two small fish. . .but what would so little do in the face of so much need?" His voice sounded uncertain yet almost hopeful, as if he wanted to believe something that he knew was beyond his reach.

Jesus looked at Andrew, then at Jesse. He was still sitting down, so Jesse could see him eye to eye. Jesus smiled at him— and there was that twinkle again!

"You can have it if it will help," Jesse said again. As he spoke, his stomach growled, and he put his hand on his tummy in embarrassment. That just made Jesus smile all the more.

"Thank you, Jesse. This is just what I need." Turning to Peter, he said, "Tell the people to arrange themselves in groups of fifty and one hundred, with space between them so we can reach them all."

Peter glanced at Philip with a "this doesn't make any sense but do what He says" look on his face. He walked down the hill with the others, fanning out into the crowd to repeat Jesus' instructions. In just a few minutes there were dozens of groups of people arranged like colorful flower beds against the green grass.

One of the twelve began silently counting, and when he turned to Jesus, he said, "There are at least five thousand men. If you count women and children—Lord, there must be twenty thousand people here!"

The number didn't faze Jesus. Taking Jesse's lunch from him, He smiled again and winked, like He was sharing a secret between friends. What did He mean? Jesse wasn't sure what was happening, but the look on Jesus' face made Jesse smile back. Something fun was about to happen.

Jesus stood, and the crowd instantly quieted. Taking Jesse's little bundle, Jesus unwrapped it and held it up above His head as He looked toward heaven. "Blessed art Thou, O Lord, our God, who brings forth bread from the earth." That was the prayer Jesse's family prayed every day. Yet the tone of Jesus' voice was so grateful and glad. . .it was as if He was talking to family.

Then Jesus brought down Jesse's bundle. . .and it was *full* of bread and fish, so full the other disciples had to catch some loaves before they fell. Jesus grinned at His helpers. "Now, men. . .let's give these people something to eat."

The twelve each had a large basket, and they began to fill them with the food from Jesse's bundle. The bread and the fish just kept coming and coming and coming. The disciples kept filling their baskets and taking food to the people with amazed looks on their faces, then refilling them and giving out fish and bread again and again, munching their own lunches as they went. Jesus reached into the bundle and handed a fish to Jesse, again with a wink and a smile.

People were laughing and eating, sharing with each other. Where there's abundance, there's no need to hoard. . .and the vast crowd found themselves in the middle of the biggest free lunch they'd ever seen. As they finished, people got up to leave, shouting their astonished thanks as they headed into the fading light of day. Jesus just smiled and waved His good-bye in return. He looked tired but very happy.

As the crowd dispersed, Jesus directed the twelve to gather up the leftovers in those large baskets. When they reconvened at the place where Jesus sat, they counted twelve full baskets of food. All his helpers looked at each other in wonder: Jesus had fed thousands with a little boy's lunch.

What do you say when God completely blows open the little box of faith where you've been living—and shows you it can be as big as the Creator's creation? Jesus just smiled. He was still holding the bundle with Jesse's lunch, and now He put His hand on Jesse's shoulder. Looking intently into Jesse's eyes, He

said, "Thank you, son. Because you were willing to give the little you had, God was able to feed many people."

Jesse looked up at Him, still overwhelmed with awe.
Because of him. . .him! Then a thought came to him with a
seven-year-old's simplicity: Wait a minute. . .

Jesus said God fed all those people. . .

but it was Jesus who multiplied his little lunch. . .

so if Jesus was the one who fed all those people, then. . .

Jesus would have to be God.

Jesse looked up at Jesus, his mouth open in a silent "ah" of
growing understanding. Earlier Jesse had put his lunch in Jesus'
hands—but now, in a simple wordless act of faith that con-
nected two hearts, he put his life in Jesus' hands.

As if He knew exactly what Jesse was thinking, Jesus gave his
shoulder a squeeze and nodded with that now-familiar twinkle in
His eyes. "Come on, Jesse, we'll walk you home. I'd like to meet
your family."

Jesus would like to meet his family?! Jesse couldn't wait to
have his family meet Jesus. The story of his rock skipping was
completely forgotten. . . . This story would change his family
forever. In fact, years later friends and family would remark that
Jesse's favorite saying was, "You can never outgive God."

Jesse suddenly realized he was holding his lunch bundle. He
looked down and saw that it now contained twice as much as
before he gave it to Jesus. Jesus took one of the loaves, broke it,
and gave Jesse half while He took a bite of the other half. Jesse
took a bite of the bread. . .and then grinned up at Jesus with a
sparkle in *his* eyes.

It was wheat.

BEYOND THE STORY
Questions to Nudge Your Thinking
and Nourish Your Heart

1. Why do people so often approach God as a taker instead of a Giver?

2. The disciples were "people tired" as they saw the large crowd representing so many concerns. Are you "people tired" right now? Get alone with Jesus and spend some time with Him. Let Him readjust your perspective and refresh your spirit. People are the reason He came!

3. Jesse could have kept his lunch all to himself—after all, it was all he had to meet his own needs. Yet he put the little he had in Jesus' hands and wound up blessing people he didn't even know. What "lunch" is in your hands that Jesus could use to help others? Will you trust Him to take care of your needs if you put it in His hands? Our sacrifice often becomes the catalyst for a miracle from God.

A New Way of Living

Now why did He say that? The thought came to James's mind but not out of his mouth. The day had already been highly unusual, and now Jesus had said one of those incredible things all the disciples knew meant far more than they could immediately understand. James also knew Jesus would cue them in if they kept their hearts and minds open.

They had started their day like most other days, rising early. They ate and then began their journey back to their home area in Galilee. That's when the unusual part of their day had started:

They traveled through Samaria to get to Galilee.

Even though it was the shortest way to make the trip, most people took the longer way around to avoid going through Samaria. The disciples were a little uneasy about traveling through what could be dangerous territory, but Jesus was definite about needing to travel through Samaria instead of around it. He almost seemed to be expecting something to happen along the way.

> The Jewish day was considered to begin at six A.M. (called "the first hour") and concluded twelve hours later at six P.M. It was also measured in three-hour periods called "watches."

The day had started hot and gotten more so as the sun rose higher. Despite the heat, their pace had been steady, and when they had been traveling on foot for nearly six hours, they came to the well at Sychar, known to many travelers. They were hot. Tired. Thirsty. Hungry. Even Jesus looked tired from the journey. As they sat down at the well, Peter felt his weariness from the bottom of his aching, dirty feet to the top of his sweaty, sun-baked head.

Somebody's stomach growled, and they looked around at each other. They were too tired to move, but they were also too hungry and thirsty not to do something about it. The well could provide them with fresh, cold water, but it was deep and they didn't have a way to draw up the water. After some discussion, they decided to head into the village nearby, where they could buy some food and something to drink. Jesus—still acting as if He knew something they didn't—told them He would wait and rest at the well while they went for the food.

As they headed down the path into the village, a woman

came toward them carrying a clay water jar on her head. Although the jar itself was fairly heavy, slow plodding steps made her seem like she was carrying the weight of the world on her shoulders. James could tell she had noticed them, but she kept her head down and did not raise her eyes to look at them. The disciples did not speak to her either, for Jewish men were not supposed to speak to a woman in public, and certainly not to a Samaritan woman. They passed each other in silence, although James thought it odd that a woman would be coming to the well in the heat of the day. Usually the women of the village came together early in the morning or at dusk to get water and chat about the events of the day. The fact that this woman was coming to the well alone and in the middle of the day told him a great deal about her relationships with the rest of her village, especially the women. This woman was obviously a social outcast. But hunger pangs tugged at James's stomach again, and he forgot the woman.

They bought their food and headed back to the well to eat lunch with Jesus. The same woman was coming toward them again, but without her water jug this time, and she looked far different from their first meeting. Instead of trudging along, she walked briskly, almost skipped. The thought occurred to James that she seemed to be walking on air. Her head was up, and her face seemed to glow. As they passed her, she looked straight at them, and although she said nothing, what James saw in her face spoke volumes. He had seen that look before in the faces of many other people who had been transformed by Jesus of Nazareth.

What James had not seen was the life-changing conversation at the well. The woman was indeed a social outcast, ostracized because of her history. She would have left her situation long ago, but she had no place else to go. Her own choices had trapped her.

She had seen the group of men as she trudged up the path to the well, but she kept her head down, hoping to avoid their notice. Noon was the only time she could go to the well. Snide comments and sullen stares from the other women in the village had long since barred her from drawing water at the regular times.

When she got to the well, she was surprised to see a Man sitting there all alone. His dress marked him as a Galilean like the other men in the group she had seen. He looked tired, but as He looked up at her, His eyes lit up, as though He had been expecting her. Trying to keep her own eyes averted, she went to the other side of the well to let down her bucket, hoping to get her water and be gone with no further notice from the Man.

Israel is only about 120 miles long from north to south. In the far north was Galilee, in the far south was Judea, and in between was Samaria. A trip from south to north through Samaria would take about three days. Taking the alternative route to avoid Samaria took twice as long. For centuries Jews and Samaritans had little to do with each other, although they were ancestral cousins racially. In fact, most Jews and Samaritans hated each other. Samaritans were those who intermarried with foreign invaders when the Kingdom of Israel was overcome, so they were of mixed bloodlines. Orthodox Jews considered them racially and religiously impure.

She felt the Man's eyes on her, but not the way she usually did when men looked her over. He almost seemed to be waiting for her to say something. She had no idea what was happening.

She brought the first bucket of water up to the top of the well and dipped some out with a ladle, letting the cool water slide down her dry throat. She could feel it all the way to her stomach.

"Give me a drink, please." His voice was deep but not demanding.

She looked up at Him, confused. This was getting stranger by the moment. Everyone knew a man could not speak in public to a woman who was not his wife. It was especially taboo for a Jewish man to say anything at any time to a Samaritan woman. What was going on here?

Her eyes on the ground in front of her, her voice low, she replied, "How it is that You, a Jew, ask a drink from me, a woman of Samaria?" Her tone attempted to end the conversation before it went any further. Men had asked her for a drink before, and she didn't want to go where those conversations had led.

She felt His eyes again, but He paused before he spoke. At last, he said, "If you only knew the gift God has for you, and who I am, you would ask Me for a drink, and I would give you living water."

Gift? God? Living water? She felt even more confused. . . and curious. None of this was making any sense at all. She stared at Him, trying to decide if something was wrong with Him. Maybe the midday sun had become too intense and He was disoriented. What she saw was an ordinary-looking man who gazed calmly back at her, waiting patiently as she tried to form a response.

She took a deep breath and tried again, speaking slowly as she tried word by word to figure out what to say. "But sir, You have no bucket and this well is very deep. Where would You get this living water?" She paused, then continued. "Besides, are You greater than our ancestor Jacob who gave us this well? Can You offer better water than he and his sons and his cattle enjoyed?"

Again the Man spoke, his voice patient. "People soon become thirsty again after drinking this water. But the water I give them takes away thirst altogether. It becomes a spring within them, gushing fountains of endless life."

Now she was more than curious. He seemed so certain of what He said. If she could have some of this water He was talking about, maybe she would no longer have to come to this well in the heat of the day. Maybe this living water would even satisfy something she had been thirsty for longer than she realized.

"Please, sir. . .give me some of that water! Then I won't ever be thirsty again." She gestured to her bucket and water jar as she said, "And I won't have to come here to haul water any more." What she left unsaid was, "And I won't have to feel the sting of being an outcast."

Again He hesitated, but this time His eyes seemed to look below her surface, as if He were able to view her memories, her thoughts. He was looking into her heart. He leaned forward slightly. "Go call your husband."

It was a simple request, but the words pried wide the door to her life. Why would He say that of all things?

She shifted uncomfortably, unable to meet his gaze. "I don't have a husband." The words sounded evasive. They were.

"You're right." His words were penetrating, convicting. . . but not condemning. "You've had five husbands, and you aren't married to the man you are living with now."

How could he have known that? This Man knew far more

about her than she wanted anyone to know. How could he put his finger so quickly and easily on the real reason she was coming to the well at noon? How could he uncover her shame? She deserved her reputation. . .she had earned it. She had tried to satisfy her thirst for love with the cheap substitute of physical intimacy and the material provision a man represented—any man. A string of failed relationships had only intensified her yearning for unconditional love.

This was getting way too close to home. She had to divert this conversation before it got any more personal than it already was. Wait a minute. The Man had mentioned God. Maybe she could talk about religion. That would get them on different. . . safer. . .ground.

"Sir, You must be a prophet to be able to say these things. Since You are religious, tell me this. Why do you Jews insist on worshipping only a certain way at a certain place? You say Jerusalem is the right place to worship, while we Samaritans claim it is here at Mount Gerizim where we have always worshipped, just as our ancestors did." There. That ought to do it. These Jews always liked a good theological debate. If she got him talking about religious rituals and such, she would be safe.

The Man smiled as if He knew exactly what she was trying to do, but His words were not defensive or unkind. "You Samaritans know so little about the One you worship, while we Jews know all about Him, for salvation comes through the Jews. Believe me, though, the time is coming when it will no longer matter whether you worship the Father here or in Jerusalem. Who you are and the way you live are what count with God. True worship engages your spirit in the pursuit of truth. The Father is looking for anyone who will worship Him that way;

He wants people who will simply and honestly be themselves before Him in their worship. For God is Spirit, so those who worship Him must worship in spirit and truth—out of their very being, their spirits, their true selves, in adoration."

He wasn't arguing with her. He was teaching her and inviting her to a deeper understanding at the same time. His gentle truth was reaching places in her heart she thought she had long since barricaded with guilt, pain, doubt, and confusion. Obviously, He knew all about her, yet He had not rejected her like everyone else who knew what she'd done. He called God "Father"; He said the Father was looking for people who would worship Him in spirit, not in a prescribed ritual; He said the Father was looking for people who would worship Him in truth. That required honesty, a quality she had been running away from too long. She had yearned for security, but she had traded her dignity to get it. If she could really experience this gift the man was talking about. . .if her parched spirit could really drink until her heart's thirst was quenched. . .

She knew enough about religion to know that God had promised to send Someone someday who would make God understandable, knowable, reachable. This person—the Messiah —He was supposed to be the answer for Jews and Samaritans alike. That was one of their few points of common ground. Maybe this Man could tell her more about this Messiah. Maybe this was what she'd been looking for all along.

"I do know that we both believe the Messiah will come," she said, "the One who is called the Christ. When He comes, He will explain everything to us." She heard her voice shake. This man had taken only about five minutes to get to the deepest issues of her life. Her need made her tremble. What was it about this Man that was completely shaking her world?

He must have seen the pleading in her eyes. . .must have heard the cry of her heart. He had to see. He had seen everything else about her. He walked over to her, and she looked down at the ground, afraid to meet His gaze. He didn't reach out and touch her, but she felt him touching her heart.

"You're looking for the Messiah to bring you the answers to your life."

She nodded, unable to speak.

"You're talking to Him."

She looked up, her eyes wide with wonder. *Yes. . .who else could have known. . .how else could He have known? Who else would take the time to talk to a soiled woman and offer her a gift only God could provide? Who else could talk about God with such familiarity and intimacy? Who else. . .*

He smiled and nodded, as if He were listening to her thoughts. "Yes. I am the Messiah."

All she had longed for in a man. . .all she had yearned for in God. . .was standing here before her. He asked nothing of her. He gave her everything she had ever needed. Her face lit up with joy; her heart felt as if a spring of pure, clean, *living* water had opened up inside, cleansing her, refreshing her. She was clean!

"I've got to tell the others! I've got to tell them!" She ran down the path to the village, forgetting her water bucket and jar. She wasn't thirsty anymore. . .and at the deepest level of her life, she never would be again.

When the disciples reached the well, Jesus was still sitting there, but He was looking refreshed and content. Sitting down, they began to devour the food they brought, but Jesus made no move to join them. For a couple of minutes they concentrated on consuming as much bread and cheese as they could in a short amount of time. Then James looked over at Jesus, who was watching them with a hint of amusement. James's chewing slowed, and he nudged his brother, John. One by one, the disciples turned to watch the Master. Suddenly self-conscious, they all stopped chewing.

"Master, You need to eat something. We've brought plenty of food. . .please, eat," James said. The rest murmured their agreement.

Jesus smiled at them, that I-know-something-you-need-to-know smile they had seen many times before. "I have food to eat that you men know nothing about. . .yet," He said. That was when the thought came to James: *Now what does He mean by that?* Had someone brought Him something to eat already? He had not seen the woman carrying any food with her, and he had seen no one coming up the path to the well. . .so what did Jesus mean?

Again Jesus smiled. He leaned forward, looking at each one of His puzzled disciples, who had completely forgotten the food that had been so important just a minute before. "Do you want to know what really nourishes and energizes Me? My food is doing the will of Him who sent Me. . .that's food and life for Me."

Then He stood up and pointed down the path to the village. As their eyes turned, they saw the woman coming back up the path. This time she was not alone. Dozens and dozens. . . hundreds of people came with her. The entire community was headed toward the well to meet Jesus. They, too, wanted the Living Water that would satisfy their deepest needs.

Pointing at the crowd of people, Jesus said, "Do you not usually say, if you plant the seed you have to wait at least four months for harvest? Look! Open your eyes, men! There is a great harvest of souls all around us, and the fields are white and ready to harvest now."

Then James began to understand why Jesus had been so refreshed when they returned. Jesus had the power to change people's lives—and people were His top priority. He had planted the seed of faith in one unlikely woman, a woman unacceptable to virtually everyone but Him. Now that seed was going to bear fruit. . .hundreds of lives before the day was through.

The Master stepped forward past His disciples to welcome the crowd coming toward Him. He looked eager to meet them. After a moment, James stepped forward to stand beside his Master, his eyes sparkling with anticipation. He had completely forgotten about the rest of his lunch; something far more satisfying was about to happen.

Then another thought came to his mind: I might not always understand what Jesus is doing or everything He says. But I do know this—

whatever He does, I want to be a part of it!

BEYOND THE STORY
*Questions to Nudge Your Thinking
and Nourish Your Heart*

1. Why does "religion" create such a barrier in people's conversations?

2. To reach out to the Samaritan woman, Jesus overcame several barriers—ethnic, cultural, religious, among others. What are some of the barriers you need to overcome as you attempt to reach out to others?

3. Notice the influence of one changed life. What does that tell you? What does God want to do through your life? Think about this promise from Jeremiah 29:11 (NIV): *"For I know the plans I have for you,"* declares the Lord, *"plans to prosper you and not to harm you, plans to give you hope and a future."*

4. Jesus said a great harvest of souls is all around us, ready to harvest now. What are you doing to bring in the harvest? What are some ways you can be more involved in God's great harvest field of people in need of Him?

Seeing Lessons from a Blind Man

The midmorning sun had risen and began to spread its warmth over the city of Jericho. Just outside the city gate, a man shuffled along the road, his cane tapping in front of him. His dark leathery skin felt the sun's warmth, but his eyes could not tell whether it was midnight or high noon. He had never seen the light of the sun, nor had he seen the brilliant blue sky, the puffy white clouds, the green palm trees along the road, or any of the other sights that make life so vivid and fascinating.

Bartimaeus was blind—born blind, the son of a blind man. His sightless eyes stared unfocused ahead as his cane and his ears directed him to his usual spot beside the road where he would spend the day. His only means of supporting himself was to do what many did in his condition—beg.

He was not alone. Blindness was widespread in that part of the world where unsanitary habits spread contagious eye diseases easily. His condition was all too common.

Bartimaeus sank wearily onto his spot on the ground. From there, his finely tuned hearing picked up things most people missed; he was keenly aware that blindness was not limited to the physical sphere of life. He heard the moral blindness of the merchant cheating a customer out of some money, men and women gossiping about others, committing murder with their tongues. His heart broke as he heard parents fighting, children hurting, families divided. And then there were those who called themselves religious but

Jericho was known both for its history and infamy. It had been the site of the famous "march around the walls" by the people of Israel under the direction of Joshua. Those walls tumbled from the inside out, knocked down by a shout of faith and the unseen hand of God...a great military and spiritual victory for the Israelites as they took possession of the promised land. In Jesus' time, Jericho had become famous because of the lavish winter palace Herod had built there, where he ruled with his iron will and iron fist. Most of the twenty thousand priests and as many Levites who served at the Temple in Jerusalem also lived there when they were not on duty. In the midst of the wilderness of Judea, the city's beautiful palm trees made it a refuge sought by many, and it proudly owned the title of the longest continuously inhabited city in the world.

had no compassion for others. Blinded by their own sin, they talked about God, while they lived as if He didn't exist.

Yes, so many are blind in so many ways, he thought. *At least I know I am blind.*

The offerings in his basket should be good today, anyway. It was Passover time, and the road would be filled with pilgrims going the fifteen miles to Jerusalem for the feast and worship. They would probably be feeling generous, stopping to drop a few coins to make themselves feel better before they continued on their way.

The people passed along as the hours went by, and Bartimaeus was not disappointed. Nothing special happened, until Bartimaeus's ears picked up the sound of an unusually large group of people approaching. The crowd brought with it an electric excitement that told Bartimaeus something special was going on. As the people drew nearer, he realized they were listening to the words of a teacher as He walked along. That was not uncommon. What was out of the ordinary, even extraordinary, was the laughter and outright spirit of joy that filled the air. Bartimaeus had to find out more.

He groped through the air until he grabbed someone's sleeve. "Who is it? Who is coming? Why does He have such a different spirit about Him? Who is He?"

"Why, haven't you heard?" came the reply. "Jesus of Nazareth is passing by."

Jesus of Nazareth. Bartimaeus had heard about Him for months. They said wherever He went, miracles followed. And never had people heard a Man who could speak the truth of God's Word so simply and clearly. Some said He was a prophet, some said He was nothing more than a carpenter. Others said He was a danger to the nation, stirring up controversy. Many were even calling Him the Messiah—no one could do the miracles He did, nor teach as He did, and even raise the dead back to life, unless He were indeed God's Chosen One. Others saw Him as a rebel against Rome—or against the current religious system that was ruled by the Pharisees.

Bartimaeus had heard all the opinions, but to a desperate man, opinions mattered little. Perhaps this was his chance. This Man had made others see; Bartimaeus had even talked to some of them.

It was now. . .or maybe never.

Bartimaeus made his decision. No matter what anyone else did, he was going to somehow let Jesus know about His need. The crush of the crowd was so great that he could not even get to his feet, but taking his staff, he began to wave it wildly above his head, hoping Jesus would see it above the crowd. "Jesus! Son of David! Have mercy on me! Jesus! Son of David! Have mercy on me! Jesus! Have mercy on me!" He was crying out to a Man he'd never met, using titles reserved for the Messiah. He didn't know all he needed to know about Jesus—but he knew enough to yearn for the power that had changed others.

Those around him tried to hush him. "Be quiet!" they said. "He's too busy for such a one as you. Be quiet so we can hear Him."

But a desperate man could not be silenced so easily. His voice became louder, more frantic. "Jesus! Son of David! Have mercy on me! Please, Jesus! Have mercy on me!"

Although Bartimaeus couldn't see Him, the Man at the center of the crowd stopped. His eyes swept across the teeming mass of people until they came to rest on the tip of a waving cane. In a voice filled with tenderness and welcome, He said, "Call him and bring him here to Me."

The tone of those around Bartimaeus changed immediately. "Cheer up!" they said. "He's calling for you." Throwing off his old cloak, Bartimaeus sprang to his feet; leaving his cane behind, he followed the hands of the people who formed a narrow path to the Master.

As he grabbed calloused carpenter's hands, he sensed this Man's strength. Instinctively, he tipped his face up toward the Lord's.

"What do you want Me to do for you?" asked Jesus. Some in the crowd looked at each other with their eyebrows raised; wasn't it obvious what this man needed? Why would Jesus ask such a silly question?

Bartimaeus did not think it was a foolish question. "Rabbi. . . Master, I want to see!" Oh, how long he had wanted to tell someone that and not be disappointed. He grasped both of Jesus' hands tightly, not wanting to let Him get away.

The great crowd of people was silent, hanging on every word between the blind man and Jesus. They had been listening to His teaching—but could Jesus validate His words with something so wonderful as an answer to a blind man's request?

Jesus looked into Bartimaeus's sightless eyes as if He were looking into the thoughts and intents of his heart. "Go," He said softly as He smiled. "Your faith has healed you."

As soon as the words were spoken, the utter darkness Bartimaeus had seen all his life began to fade to gray. . .and then as if a blindfold had been removed, Bartimaeus's eyes focused. . . and he could see! The very first sight he ever saw, one forever etched on his mind, was the face of Jesus Himself. The Master's eyes danced with joy, wet with tears.

"I can see! I can see!" Bartimaeus cried. Oh, the beauty of it all! The sun, the sky, the amazed faces of the people, and best of all, the face of Jesus. The crowd erupted into a great cheer, overwhelmed with the event that had taken place in front of their eyes. However, some eyes bleak with malice moved off to report to the ones who in a few days would seek Jesus' death.

For a moment the crowd was motionless, caught up in the miracle, and then they surged forward again as the Master continued on His journey to Jerusalem. But there was one more follower with that group of disciples, Bartimaeus by name, a blind man no more. As they traveled, he gleefully told over and over the story of how Jesus had given him sight.

We can all learn from the faith of Bartimaeus. He was persistent. He came as soon as Jesus called him, not waiting until he had all the theological answers figured out. He didn't even fully understand who Jesus was, but he knew enough to put his life completely in Jesus' hands. . .and that was all Jesus was looking for. Bartimaeus's faith healed him, but only because he put his faith in Jesus. Once Jesus met his need, he showed his gratitude by following Jesus, and then others could see his faith in his thankful life.

We all need "seeing" lessons from this once-blind man. When we look through his eyes—the eyes of faith—we can see everything. Blessed are those who "see". . .and believe.

Do you *see*?

BEYOND THE STORY
*Questions to Nudge Your Thinking
and Nourish Your Heart*

1. Blindness comes in many forms. What are some of the types of blindness you saw in this story? What are some of the types of blindness in our culture today?

2. Bartimaeus didn't have all his theological facts learned before he looked to Jesus in faith. When could making sure we "have the right theology" become a hindrance to genuine faith?

3. When you look at Jesus, what do you *see*?

4. What new lessons about faith did you learn from Bartimaeus? How can you put those lessons into practice right now?

Jesus Comes Late
. . .Just in Time

Jesus was late. . .and Lazarus was dead.

Watching Martha stand there with tears streaming down her face broke my heart. Her brother was dead and buried. I'd seen Jesus in many situations, but I'd never before seen Him intentionally delay when faced with an urgent need. This just wasn't like Him. The bewilderment in Martha's eyes mirrored the thoughts in my mind. Why? Why did Jesus choose to wait when Lazarus's life was hanging in the balance? Because Jesus hadn't come in time, Lazarus was dead. The one whose name meant "God is my help" received no help when he needed it most.

We had been across the Jordan River in the village of Bethabara, where John had preached and baptized so powerfully before his untimely death. Just as they had with John, people streamed into the barren area, like a new tributary flowing toward the Jordan. The people knew Jesus was the source of the miracles they thirsted for, and as He always did, Jesus touched and transformed every needy heart that came to Him. Like always, He treated each person as if they were the most important one in the world. I never grew tired of watching Jesus doing supernatural things in such a natural way. It wasn't second nature to Him. . .it *was* His nature.

In the midst of that busy scene a young man arrived, carrying a short but urgent message from Mary and Martha of Bethany: "Lord, the one You love is sick. . .and sinking." The implication was obvious: We need You, and we need You *now*. If You come, You can heal our brother like You've healed so many. The twenty-mile distance from Bethabara to Bethany could be traveled in one long day of nonstop walking. If we hurried. . .

Jesus smiled at the messenger. He told him the sickness would not result in grieving and death but would bring glory to the Son of God. Telling him not to worry, Jesus sent him back to the sisters. He seemed to know something we didn't, but He did not tell us what it was. We all got to our feet, expecting Him to signal our departure.

But instead, Jesus continued to center His attention on the crowd that surrounded Him. He acted as if He had all the time in the world to respond to the urgent summons. I thought it was odd at the time, especially since Jesus loved that family so much.

Although Mary, Martha, and Lazarus were people of means, they had been followers of the simple carpenter from Nazareth almost from the beginning. Their house became "home" for Jesus when we were in Jerusalem, and since they lived only two miles away from the city, just across the Kidron Valley on the slope of the Mount of Olives, it was the perfect base for us. We had spent many pleasant meals there, laughing together as sunlight splashed across the table through the window, telling stories and sharing our hearts until lengthening shadows let us know evening had come. Jesus found their home an oasis of friendship in the midst of His busy ministry. Martha always had a great meal ready, Mary loved to just sit at Jesus' feet and listen to Him, and Lazarus treated Jesus like a brother. Most places we went, people were either constantly asking something from Jesus or actively opposing Him. That home in Bethany was one of the few places where Jesus was loved without His having to do anything at all; just being Himself was enough.

We had not been to visit them in Bethany recently, because the last time we were in Jerusalem, the Pharisees had stirred up so much anger toward Jesus that people were ready to stone him. Jesus had defused the situation, and we left without further incident, but we were not eager to put ourselves anywhere near that kind of danger again. So I guess in a way we were all relieved that we wouldn't be going to Bethany after all.

Two evenings passed, and still Jesus continued to care for the people there in Bethabara, but I sensed He was waiting for something. On the morning of the third day after the request for aid from Bethany, He turned to us and said in a matter-of-fact tone, "Men, let's go back to Judea."

We all looked at each other uneasily, and my stomach began to churn. Judea meant Jerusalem. Jerusalem meant danger, possibly death. Sick friend or not, all of us clearly understood the implications of Jesus' words. For a moment we were silent, looking at the ground. Andrew drew a ragged circle in the dirt with his sandal.

Finally Peter, as usual, spoke up. This time he spoke a bit more slowly than normal, as if trying to reason with Jesus. "Rabbi. . .the last time we were there, the Jews tried to stone You. Are You sure you want to go back there?"

All eleven of us nodded in agreement, each of us murmuring our assent to Peter's words. Jesus had healed people without actually being present before. Couldn't He do it again in this present scenario? It seemed to make a lot more sense to answer the prayer of the sisters from a distance.

Jesus looked at us with a twinkle in His eyes. We couldn't fool him. Here were His twelve disciples, occasional fearless men of faith, now acting more like a bunch of scared schoolboys. He smiled. "Aren't there twelve hours of daylight? As long as we walk in the light, we won't stumble and fall." Clearly, Jesus was headed back to Bethany with His eyes wide open, unafraid because He knew He was walking in the light of His Father's guidance. "Besides," He added, "our friend Lazarus has fallen asleep, and I need to go wake him up."

I thought Jesus meant Lazarus was getting better, since sleep is the best doctor for a sick man. I said as much, with the other disciples again nodding their agreement.

This time Jesus stood up, and the twinkle had vanished

from His gaze. Instead, I saw a look of quiet resolve. He looked around the circle, looking each of us in the eyes before He spoke, His voice quiet but blunt. "Lazarus is dead. For your sakes I'm glad I was not there when he died." Drawing His cloak around His shoulders, He turned to go, then looked back over His shoulder. "You're about to be given new grounds for believing. Come on. . .let's go see him." Without another word, He started up the road toward Jerusalem.

We all looked at each other. We had followed Jesus every-where and anywhere, but this time. . . Thomas, the "realist" of our group, waved his hand toward our departing master and said with resignation, "Come on, men. If He's going back there to die, we might as well go die with Him." Without another word, we followed.

We said little all those twenty winding miles to Bethany. The road was a steady incline upward, almost the exact oppo-site of my attitude, which was descending into doubt. What did Jesus mean, *You're about to be given new grounds for believing?* We walked in silent, puzzled thought. The closer we got to Bethany, the more the Master's face hardened into resolve.

He looked as if He were preparing for battle.

When we got to Bethany, we stopped a short distance from the home. Since the family was well known and lived so close to Jerusalem, many people were there to pay their respects. Visits to the sick and grieving were considered an essential part of our reli-gion. I was glad to see so many mourners, because if a person was labeled an unfit "apostate" by the religious leaders (and being identified with Jesus could easily earn someone that label), mourners would stay away; those who did come would mock the dead, expressing pleasure at his or her passing.

We could hear the practiced wailing of the professional mourners. The sheer incongruity of all those hired mourners had troubled me many times, but this time was different. There

Professional mourners were common in Jesus' day. Burial took place the same day as death, with a thirty-day grieving period after the death of a loved one. The first three were called the days of weeping. Friends, family, and people hired to help with the mourning gathered at the home of the deceased. No work was done and no normal greetings were exchanged. Grief, real and contrived, was heard, seen, and tasted all the way down to the bitter food eaten by the mourners. People were expected to express their grief in tangible ways, sometimes to the point of extravagance. Rich people such as Martha and Mary's family were often more concerned about the appearance of their mourning than missing the one who died. Death became a surreal opportunity to prove one's worth before a watching community. Trips to the grave were led by women, since it was believed that death came to humanity through the sin of Eve. There the wailers chanted loud songs of grief. Friends and well-wishers spoke praises on behalf of the dead person between the funeral songs. The spirit of the person, they believed, hovered near for three days and would appreciate the kind words spoken.

On the fourth day things changed. The bitter gall of death had now changed the face of the deceased, and the spirit left to its final place. At that point, all hope was gone. Seven days of lamentation began. Some people carried things to an extreme—women pulled out their hair, men sometimes scourged themselves to prove the intensity of their sorrow. Most just laid in their beds for days in torn clothes without cleansing or anointing themselves.

Death came often in Jesus' land, and death deserved proper respect. Death was a dark and hopeless chasm. The elaborate rituals were designed to allow people to look over the eternity's edge enough to realize death's enormity, express their grief on behalf of the one who had just fallen into its dark pit. . .and then return to life as before, living as if nothing of eternal significance had happened.

was something about the way Jesus was approaching all this that made it unlike any death scene I'd ever seen before.

We stood there for a few moments before someone noticed us and approached. I recognized the messenger who had brought us his message four days ago. He came up to Jesus and spoke in a low voice, filling us in on the details of the past days. Lazarus had died that same day while the messenger was on his way to us at Bethabara. Lazarus had been in the tomb four days already. The days of weeping were over; the week of lamentation had begun. Jesus spoke kindly to the man, thanking him for his effort to help his friend, and told him to ask Martha and Mary to meet Him outside the house, away from the crowds. The man turned back toward the house, his slow steps and sloping shoulders a silent portrait of sorrow and hopelessness.

After a few moments, we saw Martha coming toward us, dressed in dark clothes and despair. She looked awful. Black shadows hung below her red-rimmed eyes, and her face was tearstained and strained from sleeplessness. Without a word she fell into Jesus' arms and clung to Him, her head on His shoulder, her shoulders shaking silently as she began to weep again. Jesus just held her, His embrace speaking more than words could, resting His cheek on her head as she wept.

Finally Martha stepped back, still holding Jesus' hands, and looked up at Him, her face a mixture of bewilderment and trust. Her voice strained from days of weeping, she said, "Lord, if You would have been here, my brother would not have died." She heaved a great sigh as she fought the tears. "But. . .even now I know that God will give You whatever You ask. . . ." Her words hung in the air. . .an invitation, a wish, words that spoke of hope when all hope was gone, a prayer she desperately yearned to be more than wistful presumption. She looked up at Him earnestly, as if searching for an answer to her unlikely petition. We all just stood there, shock on our faces. In one breath Martha had accused Jesus of allowing her brother to die—and then turned around and asked Him to raise Lazarus from the dead!

Jesus looked deep into Martha's eyes with no hint of reproach at her words, only sympathy and understanding. "Your brother will rise again."

That was the "correct" thing to say, and Martha gave the "correct" response: "Yes Lord, I know. Everyone will be raised up on the resurrection day in the end."

That's where most conversations at funerals ended: polite, correct phrases designed to provide superficial comfort, insulation against the emotional trauma of the moment. I'd heard these words many times before. . .but this was Jesus, and where most conventional conversations ended, His usually began. I leaned forward to hear what He would say next.

He put His hands on Martha's shoulders, still looking deep into her eyes, and He must have seen something: a flicker of faith in the midst of the confusion and grief, trust instead of despair. What He said next changed my attitude about death forever.

"Martha. . .*I am* the resurrection and the life. Whoever believes in Me will live even if he has died, and whoever believes in Me will never die in the end. Do you believe this, Martha?"

There was something about how He said the words *I am.* I had heard Him say those words when He was walking on a boiling sea in the midst of a howling storm. I had heard them said to a group of pompous Pharisees: "Before Abraham was even born, *I am.*" Suddenly God's words to Moses so many centuries ago came alive for me: "Tell them *I AM* has sent you. . . ." Jesus. . .the great *I AM*. . .God Almighty. Death has no power in the presence of the Author of life—and Martha was looking full in His face.

The look on her face changed, and I could tell her heart was absorbing and welcoming the truth. Hope rang in her voice now as she said, "Yes, Lord. . .I have always believed that You are the Messiah, the Son of God who has come into the world. I believe. . . . I've got to tell Mary!"

With that she turned and hurried back to the house. We watched Martha call her sister to the doorway, whisper in her ear, point to us. Mary hurried toward us, the crowd following close behind, some curious at her abrupt departure, some concerned.

When she was close to us, she burst into tears and collapsed at Jesus' feet, as if unloading an unbearable burden. How many times had she sat at those feet, drinking in His every word? How many times had her heart thrilled to the truth she heard from His lips? How many times had she told him she would trust him regardless of what might happen? Now she didn't know what to think. Her trust was undergoing the ultimate test. Could she. . .would she trust Him, even when He was too late to help her brother?

I could barely understand her words as she huddled there on the ground, her voice thickened with heartache. "Lord, if You would have been here, my brother would not have died." With that Mary wept deep, wrenching, heaving sobs that left her gasping for breath. As the crowd saw her cry, they, too, broke into feigned tears, making the whole scene a bizarre cacophony.

Jesus knelt down and gently brought Mary to her feet, His arms wrapped protectively around her. His eyes filled with tears. Then He looked around at the counterfeit grief on the faces of the crowd, tears for show rather than sympathy for the woman in his arms, and anger flashed across His face. Standing next to Him, I heard Him groan out loud as He stood in the swirling vortex of emotions. The air was heavy with hopelessness, almost taunting us. We all stood there helpless. . .speechless. There was literally nothing we could do. Death had won.

But as I watched Jesus' face, I realized He was listening to things we could not hear, things not discernable to the human ear, things being spoken from the shadows of the spirit realm. His face grew hard again, as it had earlier when we were on the road to Bethany. I knew the battle He had been preparing for was here.

Martha had joined us by then, and Jesus put His arms around both women, each weeping on a shoulder, their tears soaking His cloak. Turning to the young messenger, He said in a low voice that was firm with authority, "Where have you put him?"

They led us to the tomb. It was like most tombs—a cave carved out of the pale limestone so common in that area. A large rock fashioned into a stony wheel had been rolled in front of the opening.

Mary and Martha looked up into Jesus' face with tears streaming down their faces. Their look was so forlorn and pitiful that we all began to cry. Jesus looked down at them. . .and then He drew them close to His heart and wept with them, tears running down His face and into His beard.

For a long moment all we could do was cry. The crowd hovered around us, and I caught the whispers being passed one to another.

"See how much Jesus loved him." "Yes, but this Man made the blind to see. Why couldn't he keep Lazarus from dying?"

Again I could tell Jesus was hearing more than my natural ears could discern. He groaned deeply again, and this time it was almost like the low growl of a lion facing an enemy.

"Roll away the stone."

We all heard Him, but no one moved in response.

Martha tipped her head back to look up at Jesus. "But Lord, he's been dead for four days, and by this time the odor will be awful."

Jesus cupped her cheek with his callused carpenter's hand and wiped away her tears with His thumb. He smiled a reassuring smile down at Martha, then at Mary. "Didn't I tell you that if you would believe, you would see the glory of God?" The question was gentle, nudging Martha back to the faith she had spoken only moments ago. Slowly she nodded, looked to the tomb and then back at Jesus. Her eyes large with growing understanding, she nodded again.

Motioning to the men near the entrance of the tomb, Jesus bid them again to roll away the heavy stone, revealing the black opening to what was the final resting place of Lazarus's body.

Jesus stepped past the two sisters to the front of the tomb. They clung to each other, eyes wide. The crowd grew quiet, sensing something beyond anything they had ever seen at a graveside.

Jesus looked up into the sky and lifted His hand in what appeared to be a gesture of familiar greeting. His face softened with love, and He spoke to an Audience of One, yet loud enough that everyone in the crowd could hear, "Father, thank You for hearing Me. You always hear Me, but I'm talking out loud for the sake of all these people so they might believe You have sent Me."

Then Jesus lowered His arm and pointed straight into the black depths of the tomb. . .and the depths beyond. His smile faded into a stern resolve. The Author of life was taking authority over the ruler of death.

"Lazarus!" Jesus' voice was a loud command, ringing with supernatural authority. "Come out!"

I was holding my breath. The crowd was so still we could hear the chirp of a small bird in the distance. . .and then the sound of shuffling in the tomb. First we saw a hand gripping the edge of the entrance—and then Lazarus filled the doorway!

He was wrapped in strips of cloth, neck to feet, like every dead body, with a napkin tied around his chin to keep his mouth closed. He blinked into the sunlight, then looked around, straight into the face of Jesus. Suddenly his face lit up.

I was not looking into the emaciated face of a four-day-old corpse. The man I saw in front of me was flushed with life. Jesus stepped forward, Lazarus struggled against his wrappings, Martha and Mary were running—and suddenly two sisters, a brother, and the Savior were embracing, all four weeping. . .this time with tears of joy.

The crowd erupted into spontaneous cheers. Everyone was talking at once, too amazed to know what to say, too overwhelmed with wonder to stay silent.

A dead man. . .alive!

Death. . .defeated!

Despair. . .cheated!

The entire scene was bathed in light beyond mere sunshine; we were literally basking in the glory of God.

Jesus looked up into heaven, His face still wet with tears of joy, and nodded His thanks. Then He said to the men who had moved the stone, "Get him out of these grave clothes. Let's get this man home." With those words the crowd cheered again.

A moment later a resurrected brother with a borrowed cloak was walking arm in arm with his sisters. . .home.

We still face the dark chasm of death today; it is the ultimate reality we all must face. It haunts us from the shadows and taunts us with its threats. None of us can escape.

Unless. . .

Unless Someone who has tasted death and overcome it on our behalf calls our name. When we answer that call, death becomes only the doorway into eternity with the Author of life. In Jesus, death's shadows can't hurt us. They disappear in the light of the Son.

Lazarus heard Jesus call his name, and he walked into His embrace, into a life that will never end.

Jesus is calling your name. . . .

Are you coming?

BEYOND THE STORY
*Questions to Nudge Your Thinking
and Nourish Your Heart*

1. We live in a culture that avoids dealing with death at all costs. Why?

2. Can you think of times in your life when God didn't answer according to your plan and later you realized He had something much better in mind? What were they? What did you learn as you look back at those situations with a better perspective?

3. What did you learn from Jesus as you watched Him respond to Martha and Mary's grief? How can that help you when you reach out to people in crisis?

4. The heart of Christianity is in the Cross and the Resurrection. A Christian's view of death should be completely different because we know that Jesus defeated death forever. Take time now to thank Jesus for His resurrection victory. . .the security we have in this life and the certainty of heaven beyond!

The Short Man's Savior

The fragrance of balsam and roses hung in the moist spring air over the "City of Palms." Jericho was even noisier than usual. Along the road toward Jericho, a small band walked toward the city, but it was quickly joined by people streaming to meet them, swelling into a crowd of hundreds. What had been a small group hardly a dozen strong became a procession. As they entered the city, the narrow streets, already crowded with vendors selling their wares, shoppers browsing, children playing, and dogs barking, became a wall-to-wall milling throng of people.

Pharisees were a Jewish religious party made mostly of middle class businessmen. Their name came from a word that meant "to separate." They believed every area of life should be governed by the Scriptures, but they wrote many of their own interpretations and additions in the form of religious regulations. They were proud of their traditions and teachings, and they looked down on those who did not live like them. Although the Pharisees were extremely exact in their outward religious appearance, Jesus frequently pointed out the perversion of their heart motives. As a result, they were always looking for a way to discredit and condemn Him.

The focus of all the attention was a Man in simple clothing. There was little out of the ordinary about Him at first glance, until you got close enough to really see Him. Then you saw the way He carried Himself—unpretentious, yet with a regal quality, unimpressed with those of status, yet accepting of all. His face held an unusual openness and a unique depth. This Man seemed to be able to look right through people and know their innermost hearts. And wherever He went, Jesus of Nazareth seemed to gather a crowd.

The crowd was an interesting mixture of people. Children laughed and spoke His name, "Jesus," as they hung on their parents' robes. Men and women who would only be described as common, ordinary folk looked at Jesus with glad, open faces. Some talked to each other of the stories they had heard about Him: blind people seeing again, sick children healed and returned to their folks, notorious sinners radically transformed. They said demons obeyed Him, and even the wind and the waves listened to His voice!

Others in the crowd were not excited participants. They were skeptical, sullen observers in the long robes of Pharisees. They were hoping to see an error or sin they could use against Jesus. After three years, they were still looking.

Up the street a man turned to see what all the excitement was about. His clothes and the rings on his fingers all suggested great wealth. His beard was neatly trimmed, and his dark, beady eyes peered out from under bushy eyebrows. He was short, and one got the impression he was always trying to make up for it. Perhaps that was why Zacchaeus had been willing to become a tax collector; it was one of the few ways a man could become wealthy, if he played his cards right. Although his name meant "pure," he had certainly sacrificed many things on his way to the top. He no longer lived up to his name.

He paid a price for his wealth, but Zacchaeus held those who rejected him in contempt. He would show them! He would acquire all his heart desired, and then he would be accepted and happy.

Over the course of time (and with his ability to use tax laws to his personal advantage), he had it all: the riches, the servants, the home others envied, the clothes, the ability to purchase whatever pleasure appealed to him at the moment. So why was he still empty and unhappy? No amount of money or power ever seemed to fill the emptiness inside him. He felt. . .well, as strange as it seemed, he felt lost. He didn't know where he was going or how to get there. He felt alone and alienated, unloved and not worth much, in spite of his many possessions. He had wrapped up his whole identity in what he could purchase, and now he found himself still wanting, wondering who he really was with or without his wealth.

"What's going on? Why all the excitement?" he asked a boy running by.

"Jesus of Nazareth is coming!"

Jesus. Like everyone else, Zacchaeus had heard all the stories about Him. And one thing had impressed Zacchaeus even more than the tales of healing, power, teaching, and forgiveness: One of Jesus' disciples was a former tax collector. The stories of Levi and his incredible change had gone through the tax collectors' grape-vine. Matthew had no more wealth, but those who knew him said he had never been happier in his life. He had nothing materially, but he lived like a man who had everything. The change in Matthew made Zacchaeus curious.

> Tax collectors were classed with murderers and thieves, because they were considered agents and collaborators with the hated Romans. Anyone contaminated by "unclean" practices or affiliated by "unclean" non-Jewish people were excluded from worshipping in the synagogue. Socially, tax collectors were outcasts, able to associate only with those of their own kind.
>
> ~

A tremendous urge to see Jesus tugged at the little man's heart. Was He all people had said? Could He possibly be the Messiah, God's Son? Could He fill the aching empty spot in Zacchaeus's shriveled heart?

By that time the front edge of the crowd had pressed him back into the doorway of his house. He tried to push his way to the front of the mob, but when people saw who he was, they pushed him back. Some kicked at him and spoke angrily to him, elbowing him out of the way. Years of being a taker had caught up with him. A wall of people stood between Zacchaeus and Jesus.

Desperate now, he ran along the edge of the crowd and found a sycamore tree. Its low branches and heavy leaves made a perfect perch for him to climb into and watch hidden as Jesus passed by. Zacchaeus settled himself on a branch to wait.

If Zacchaeus could only get a glimpse, get even a little of what had changed Levi, it might be enough. Would Jesus notice him? Would He accept him as He did Levi? Slowly Jesus approached Zacchaeus in the midst of the great crowd, until He was right below the tree Zacchaeus sat in.

Suddenly He stopped. Jesus looked straight up at the little, lonely man. One face, almost desperate in its longing; the other strong, knowing, open.

Jesus' face broke into a smile. He called up cheerfully, "Zacchaeus! Come down immediately. I must stay at your house today."

My house? My house? In this city full of priests, He wants to come to my house? Zacchaeus was frozen on his perch.

Yes! Yes! He can come to my house. I'll welcome Jesus into my home. Poor Zacchaeus almost fell out of the tree in his eagerness to get down.

The noisy crowd suddenly fell silent. Then a low voice in the background sneered, "Why, this man is a sinner. Doesn't Jesus know that good people don't associate with the likes of Zacchaeus?"

The rest of the people began to mutter, agreeing with the sentiment of the one who grumbled against Zacchaeus. Unmindful of the crowd, however, Jesus walked with Zacchaeus to his house. Reluctantly, the crowd followed along to see how Jesus would deal with a man known for cheating and cutting angles to get the best of others.

Once at the house, while servants prepared a meal for Jesus and His disciples, Zacchaeus first talked with Matthew, who had himself been a tax collector before following Jesus. Matthew's story was amazing to the ears of a tax collector such as

Zacchaeus. His heart drank in Matthew's words the way parched ground soaks up a gentle rain.

As they ate, Zacchaeus sat next to Jesus and began to spill out his heart and life to him. He sensed that Jesus knew all about him—his loneliness, his cheating, his treatment of others, his god of money—He knew it all! Christ didn't for a minute condone or accept the sin, yet Zacchaeus could not stop himself from unloading the burdens he'd carried so long. He felt ashamed in the presence of Someone who really was pure, who lived up to the name Zacchaeus could not. And yet, he could tell that the great, pure heart of Jesus actually loved him. Zacchaeus was loved! For the first time in his life, unconditional love was given and forgiveness granted.

He jumped to his feet and shouted, "I am going to give away half my wealth to the poor!" He took a deep breath and added, "What's more, I will repay fourfold all the money I cheated from people." He squared his shoulders, and his voice grew quieter. "I will make restitution. People are going to see the change in me."

Zacchaeus's life was changed that day. A new God ruled on the throne of his heart. A new purpose filled his life. A new love lifted him. He had been given a new beginning, the sins of the past were wiped clean, and he could start over again. What a day of celebration it was!

Jesus laughed for joy as He heard Zacchaeus speak, and as if to assure him and confirm his new life, He said, "Surely salvation has come to this house today. That's the whole reason I have come—to seek and to save what was lost."

Zacchaeus, tears brimming over his eyes and down his cheeks, nodded. His heart was so full he couldn't speak. That was him—lost but now found. Saved. The man who had always come up short had found a Savior.

In the days that followed, some of Zacchaeus's friends in "the business" chided him about how much money he'd given up to become a follower of Jesus. "The price is too high to follow this Man," they said. "What did He do for you that was worth that much?" Zacchaeus wasn't quite sure what to answer, but he knew his life was changed. For him, that was enough.

Months later Zacchaeus stood at the foot of a hill shaped like a skull, just outside the main gate of Jerusalem. Hanging above him, Jesus poured out His lifeblood on a rough cross. Zacchaeus stood transfixed by the sight and by the words he heard from Jesus. The last words Jesus spoke forever changed Zacchaeus's understanding of how much a human life is worth to God.

"Tetelestai!" Jesus shouted. "It is finished!" Zacchaeus recognized the word from the many business deals in which he had participated. Suddenly Zacchaeus understood what it had cost Jesus to give him forgiveness and pardon on that day when He came to Zacchaeus's house. The purchase price for his forgiveness was being paid now with Jesus' own blood. Jesus was paying with His life. The deal was done.

Now Zacchaeus had an answer for his friends when they asked him what Jesus had done for him.

All he had to do was point to the Cross.

Are you tired of trying to measure up? It didn't matter how short Zacchaeus was. It didn't matter what he had done. The ground is level at the Cross.

Listen. . . . Someone wants to come to your house.

BEYOND THE STORY
*Questions to Nudge Your Thinking
and Nourish Your Heart*

1. For many people, life's greatest unanswered question is this: "Who am I?" In our answers to this question we find our sense of identity. Look at your life. Where is your source or sources of identity?

2. Jesus ministered to "down and outers" and also "up and comers." We easily make the mistake of thinking people who look outwardly lacking are more needy than those who seem to have it all. Who do you know that seems to "have it all". . .except God? Look past the outside to the inside needs. What can you do to begin to touch those needs?

3. When he started following Jesus, Matthew had a party to introduce his friends, family, and coworkers to Jesus. A meal, comfortable surroundings, and conversation with familiar people allowed others to "see" Jesus in Matthew's life in a nonthreatening environment. Consider having a "Matthew Party" to let people you know "see" Jesus in you. Who would be on your guest list?

4. At the cross, Zacchaeus came to see the full purchase price for his forgiveness. In your heart, stand next to Zacchaeus at the foot of the cross. Ponder in awe what Jesus did for you there. . .and pour out your heart in gratitude. Better yet, let the way you live your life be your thanks to Christ.

About the Author

In his twenty years in ministry, Tim Roehl (pronounced "rail") has nurtured a passion to draw seekers and believers alike closer to Jesus Christ. So far he has published over ninety "slice-of-life" dramatic sketches designed for use in seeker-sensitive churches. Tim is also the author of *Christmas Hearts,* a collection of creatively-told stories of the first Christmas. Tim pastors ChristLife Evangelical Church—which in 1990 he helped to plant—near Minneapolis, Minnesota. He and his wife Shirley make their home nearby with their two daughters, Aubrey and Elise, and a scruffy pooch named Freeway.

Christmas Hearts

by Tim Roehl

Mary. . .Anna. . .Herod. . .the innkeeper. . .Joseph. . .
Elizabeth. They all were among the first
to glimpse Jesus, the One who was
Immanuel, the One who became God-
with-us. Now readers can glimpse Him,
too, in these creatively told
Christmastide stories. Each chapter
tells the unforgettable nativity story as
seen through the eyes of one first-
century witness. Those who saw Him
first were utterly transformed by
their encounters with their Messiah.
You will be too.